DEDICATION

To all the dandelions in the world, my beautiful disasters:
I see you.
I love you.
You are worthy.
You are a fucking masterpiece!

Who says so? I do. I am nobody, but I am somebody. That makes me worthy as it does you. To all the eyes that may lay upon this book, I appreciate you going on this journey with me. You have so many books at your disposal, and I am humbled and grateful that you chose to spend your time with my words. May they inspire you to be better, be cautious with your own words and actions, and know that one kind word, one gentle touch, one genuine compliment can make the difference between life, death, or…... revenge *wink*

I believe love & empathy truly could make the world go round. Your feelings in challenging moments are valid, but never let the darkness take over you completely. You can play in the shadows for a bit, and then I advise you to chase the sun.

Self-sabotagers……learn lessons.

Xoxo

ROTTEN FRUIT

D.W. COLE

First edition 2023
ISBN 979-8-9895071-9-1 (paperback)
ISBN 979-8-9895071-6-0 (ebook)

Cover Design by Murphy Rae, www.murphyrae.com
Editing Services provided by Ashleigh Voros and Anna Lisa Vitale of @SplitLeafSaturdays
Beta reading by Traci Finlay, www.tracifinlay.com
Beta reading by Renita Lofton McKinney, https://www.abookaday.biz/
Interior Design by Jovana Shirley, www.unforeseenediting.com

TRIGGER WARNING

Please be advised this book contains scenes (while mostly cryptic) of sexual assault, physical abuse, violence, death, and self-harm. There are also aspects of religious trauma and mental health issues present throughout the story. If you are extremely sensitive to these topics and have triggers, this may not be the right time for you to read my novella, and that's okay! I wish you all the best on your continued healing journey and please know that I sought revenge for us all with my words.

If you are in need of resources for yourself or someone you know, I have listed a few below to help you and others on the road to healing. You are not alone.

Suicide and Crisis Hotline (Spanish/English) - Call 988

https://www.iasp.info/suicidalthoughts/

https://afsp.org/

www.togetherthereishope.org

Special note: This foundation was started by my friend Kelly Cox, who is also on the Oklahoma chapter board of AFSP, in honor of her brother, Billy Clanton.

https://www.religioustraumainstitute.com/

https://www.betterhelp.com/

https://growtherapy.com/

PROLOGUE
HOT AS HELL

I OBSERVED HIM FOR *weeks before being properly equipped to face him again. Strung him along, and then I ghosted him for a few days. I needed time to tie up some loose ends and expel my rage before I finally felt composed enough to respond to his messages and calls. On the surface, he thought he had all the right actions and said all the right things to get me to return, but I remained clear in my decision to end it for good. He showed me who he was. Now it was time to show him he had no fucking clue who he betrayed. He should have just let me go, but alas, I gave in to his final plea of, "Hear me out. We can fix this, Nikki." I need closure, and tonight I am going to get it.*

Shauna, his whore of an ex, always uses her son as a line to keep him tethered. The kid isn't his, but he still pulls at his better side. At the mention of that little boy's name, his heartstrings would be played and off he'd go. Conveniently, she abandoned him and everything is suddenly clear. He knows what he wants; me. He fucked up (NO SHIT). All I have to do is play nice a little longer and then he would be free, free from the woman who carried too much baggage. A goodbye- I hate your fucking face- but you have a nice dick- remember how good you had it- now rot in hell kind of nightcap-fuck is all I am looking for. From the look on his face, the mission would be accomplished.

We dine on a home-cooked meal of his favorite dish, my special recipe of Stuffed Shells with Sauce. He is picky when it comes to the taste of his food, but he has trusted my hands to make his palette sing plenty of times in the last two years. Italian dishes that pack a little heat were often requested. I am happy to oblige, wanting him to feel this final act of love. He can't cook for shit, which is why I offered. If left up to him, we would have gone out to eat somewhere which would have been fine, but it is in my favor to have dinner here. I even went the extra mile to dig into the back of my pantry for some spices. They were hand-picked and dried years ago, so they were certain not to disappoint and would provide that extra kick. Until now, I've only allowed myself a few glasses of wine, not wanting to be out of control. I need to keep myself level-headed. No one likes an unhinged bitch when she's angry, and I know my triggers well.

When we lock eyes, I quickly glance away. While it would be perceived as being nervous, even a bit flirtatious, those of you who are like me know it is more out of necessity. Life in the real world prepared me to quickly learn, "Don't look people in the eyes for more than three seconds, or you can be viewed as a threat." It plays in the back of my mind regularly. From a pivotal age, I learned to use it to my advantage for more reasons than one. Let them think I'm scared, weak, or whatever the hell else they want. I get what I want and I'm long gone anyway. We are on the back porch where I finish a joint to calm the nerves before the real excitement ahead. He makes his way over to me and plants a kiss that makes me almost wish he isn't a piece of shit. His mouth is warm, and his tongue tastes slightly sweet with a hint of spice from when he threw back the last of one of his customary drinks; honey jack with a drop of Coke. I know his routine; I count on it.

He leads me toward the bedroom, stopping to steal another kiss and closing me against the wall with his body. I could feel his arousal against my lower stomach. Layers of clothes between us do nothing to hide his desire. Looking at where we connect with our eyes, I am grateful for his physical support. This man's smile alone makes my legs buckle. I giggle at the thought. I'll make an ass of myself looking like a damn Bambi trying to stand up straight if he lets go at this moment. Instead, I am picked up like a little fawn and wind up naked, skinned of fabric from my flesh, laid on the lower half of the bed.

"Let me see you," he says in a gentle yet lustful tone as he kneels at my bent legs and slowly parts my thighs. A sexy chuckle leaves his lips when my muscles tremble under his fingers. I lay frozen with my hands covering my belly and chest, admiring his physique; even after everything, the sight of his body still momentarily leaves me stunned. A fleeting moment of sadness crosses my mind but is quickly replaced with a vengeful arousal. Fucking me as if his life depends on it seems to be his goal. He *grabs my waist and starts bucking from the bottom, meeting me grind for grind. My hand is behind his head, holding him to my chest. He takes to my small breast like it was a DQ Blizzard and his mouth was the straw. I could feel my sensitive nipple swelling from the forced blood flow. The nerves sending twinges of pulses down my back into my legs the harder he sucked. Leaning back, I watch perfectly white teeth slide to the end of my brown nipple, he lightly nips the sensitive flesh. I adjust my hips slightly, and the next thing I know, his dick hits a spot that causes me to throw my head back in pleasure. Your girl is speaking in tongues.*

The devil himself must have entered the room at that moment. I saw flashes of colors in my peripheral vision and felt a rising heat prick my skin. I couldn't bring myself to stop the building of pleasure that was taking over my body, and my eyes closed again as it shook and trembled. I was struggling for air when the next sensation was being tossed like a rag doll across the bed and onto my stomach. I laid there momentarily, thinking he wasn't entirely done with me yet as thoughts of his release never crossed my mind; that last ride was all for me.

Commandment number seven comes across my mind. "You don't forgive because they deserve it. You forgive to keep your heart soft."

Forgive me, Father, for I have sinned......

ONE
END GAME

Every time is different, yet it is the same.

Only this time, it is different; she's in the distant plane.

The lighted path lost, but still both oars in the water.

Moving everywhere but nowhere, something has got her.

Drowning, but she still breathes air.

Motionless, yet she functions fair.

Cries for saving echo off the endless rippling surface.

She waves back as she disappears, but she is wordless.

Wickedness in her eyes is all to see.

What once was will never again be.

I don't think she will be coming back.

There is no more color; there is only black.

What will she do while I wait?

It's cruel to observe this fate.

TWO
HONOR THY FATHER

"There's a very fine line between one person's reality and
another person's fantasy."
-Conor Oberst

Bzzzzzzzzzzzz. A sound without a physical
source. My internal torment that keeps the mind at
play. The pulsing, the vibrating, and not the kind worth
stealing attention, distracts my eyes from the pages of
a badass woman who is all *ra ta ta ta*. I can always
devour this author's words, all of which contain
messages that, in their mythical way, are full of biblical
quotes and commandments, gems to help lead the
navigationally challenged such as myself. I am agitated
at having to re-read sentences more than once, unable
to focus, the light knocking on the internal door of my

psyche won't stop and every time it comes back, it's a little louder. Harder. Desperate. I squeeze my eyes tightly and breathe deeply through my nostrils, filling my lungs, quieting the sounds before they're glowing and hot; calling to come out and play.

I don't frequent this side of town. Too many people for my comfort, but shops, boutiques, and bars line each side of the two-lane road as far as the eyes travel. Street parking and the constant foot traffic on the sidewalks make it easy to blend in. I'm not too close but close enough to see the few tables that still need to be occupied as I'm sitting catty-corner to the restaurant's outside seating area which is obnoxiously cute. A sort of small, pale green and white-painted brick building that screams kale salads and overpriced tofu sits between a small boutique and the coffee shop I've inhabited. Its patio seating is blocked off by lattice wood and a mixture of potted plants, trees, and flowers of various sizes. Snapdragons are in full bloom and eating all the bees. Zinnias are striking and tall, a dance between the gentle breeze and the mirage of different oranges, pinks, and reds which display the most beautiful gentle swaying my eyes could watch perform for hours. My favorite is the honeysuckle, and if I were to pick one now I'm sure it would taste as sweet as it smells. Can see just enough through the gaps in the plants to see the benches, too.

I don't know which I'm praying for more, for him to arrive or stay away, but I am settled in for the wait. I made sure to get here early to blend in as an everyday patron; just a book lover looking for an overpriced decaf and solitude from everyday life while seeking comfort amongst the quiet chaos of strangers. Getting lost in my thoughts comes too quickly, and I am actively trying not to jump the gun. I've worked too damn hard to get here. Thankfully, reading has always been my therapy. Or maybe my escape. I don't read when I want to, only when I need to and I only "people" if I have to. Approaching me in the real world with one of my self-appointed bibles in hand is like ignoring a giant "DO NOT FEED THE ANIMALS" sign. You are doing so at your own risk. I prefer quiet and solitude for my church services. I choose reading as the last attempt to keep myself composed and from losing my shit in this coffee shop. This can't be happening…again.

It takes more work to follow Commandment number three, *"Mute & Live."* I desperately turn to her words. I am fucking triggered and on the edge. The healthy coping mechanisms I have been readily applying these last few years are nowhere in sight. My brain is ready to break. The entry is glowing and hot, my mind can hear that voice calling to come out and play again. It's been years since this has moved beyond my nightmares. It's the she-devil herself, everything I have tried my damndest to not be, breaking free from her prison I thought I successfully encapsulated her in. We have no winners here. I am mentally stuck between heaven and hell, and *she* won't let me go without a fight to the death. And so far, everything about my life seems to get scorched. The odds aren't in my favor. I'm starting to think that all those years before Wyant were one big forest fire. With time and him tending the soil, the decay and rot being transformed and fertilized, you can see the signs of life amongst my ruins. Even a few insects and animals are migrating back to graze and seeking refuge in my new grasses.

I organize my Bible into the oversized bag beside my thigh, carefully cradling it, bounded edge down, flat between the clunky wallet and black scrapbook overflowing with clippings, pictures, and papers, to keep it safe. I absentmindedly play with my phone, twirling it between my shaky hands. 12:50 PM glows back. *He should be here soon.* Glancing around, I feign composure while pretty confidently looking like I'm attending an imaginary boxing match, head swiveling at every movement that catches my eye. *Why are you here? You could be hours into Bravo TV, murder documentaries, or doing what you need to do: having service with Father Fisher while lost in the never-ending screenshots of #TWTs. Instead, you're here, like the stalking bitch you swore you'd never be again. He did this to you. You were fine. Content. He decided to pull the trigger. You're only deflecting the bullets. The odds of making it out alive or unscathed are slim when a full clip is unloaded.* I need my brain to shut the fuck up, but lately, it rarely listens.

Come on bitch, get a grip. It's just lunch, and he forgot to mention it. Stop being so damn paranoid! Go home, smoke a bowl, and CALM THE FUCK DOWN!!

"Fuck you!" I think in response to the voice in my head. The bulldog expression from the old man sitting at the table nearby tells me it wasn't in my head. She is right, though. I wish I was at the end of a bottle of whiskey and half a pack deep into Camels. It's been years since I craved the chemical-laced poison and bitter acidity that brought me so much peace before. But no, I'm fucking sitting here because people ain't shit and this man thinks I'm a fucking fool. Being a fool is one thing; you can't predict when someone will make one out of you, but being foolish is a choice. He can play me for a fool, but he will be the foolish one if he thinks he will win at this round of fuck around and find out.

He doesn't have a meeting on the calendar, his work bag is still in the home office propped up next to the doorway, the straps lying tangled together, much like the web of lies I'm starting to see, and this sure as hell doesn't look like the typical place he would take a client for lunch or even a "friend." It is too intimate, barely serves carbs, and why go all the way across town? There have to be at least a dozen places closer

11

to us downtown that serve that same insipid rabbit food. Who drives 35 minutes and sits in traffic for a fucking green juice? Cheaters. Or people with too much time on their hands, that's who.

Wyant is someone who keeps himself busy and booked. His free time is our time. Always conscious of keeping my cup filled, a delicate balance in itself. It takes precise measurements to create the desired end product. I crave solitude and peace, but I desire him more. Not just the fabulous sex; that is just a bonus. I want his presence, mind, voice, touch, everything. I am his personal science experiment he took into the lab and fine-tuned. I want no attention but all of his. Don't like long conversations and needless words filling quiet spaces, yet, he often keeps me stimulated and speaking like I am hosting a TED Talk with a time constraint to get through all my thoughts before the clock runs out. I don't like physical touch and could live without it. Still, a physical connection must be fulfilled when he is in the vicinity. Too much of one thing, I become skittish. Too little, and I become paranoid. He found the balance. Over time, with a lot of embitterment on my part, I became the cliche fairy-tale believing, lovestruck, "pick me" bitch in society that I spent years making fun of.

However, his actions of late ain't adding up; the math isn't math-ing. My gut tells me he is planning on making, or has made, a choice that will ruin us both. I can feel the unstable, potentially volatile mixtures of the head and heart swirling together, ready to combust. There isn't a scientist in the world who can predict how the hell Wyant's newly mixed concoction will react.

Everything was fine until last week.

THREE
ALWAYS PREPARE FOR WAR

Five-finger discounts have expanded to other appendages.

Help me, Mother.

Nothing.

My entire being hinges on this.

One last try; it's not too late.

It's me or him.

I lost.

But she took the bait.

This could have been a different story.

Instead unfolded a scene so gory.

Lifeless bodies and broken dishes.

Granted were my deepest wishes.

The cross I bear has me shook.

It's all my fault.

All in this book.

Do written confessions release me of sins?

This seems like the end.

No one wins.

FOUR
TRIGGERED

"There are wounds that never show on the body that are deeper and more hurtful than anything that bleeds."
- Laurell K. Hamilton

NOTHING SEEMED SUSPICIOUSLY OFF at first. Maybe on the phone a little more than usual, stepping out for private conversations or impromptu lunch meetings which disrupted our plans to sit home and do our normal more than I liked. I chalked it up to additional stress from work before we were to leave for a cruise to the Caribbean the following week. I met most of his family only a handful of times over the last few years, as they live in Louisiana and barely visit. His younger sister, Lani, lives about an hour and a half away in Virginia Beach. She, Wyant, and I planned to fly out together and meet the rest of their family in Ft. Lauderdale. Palm to face. On a boat, in the middle of the fucking ocean, with nowhere to run. At 30, this would be my first trip for pleasure. Honestly, I'd be just fine with staying home; group functions are not my thing, but Wyant promises there will be an equal time of interactions, group excursions, and solitude. I don't want to be rude to his family, but I also cannot spend all day, every day, with them. It's not them, it's me. I get depleted and overstimulated after being in their presence for more than a few hours.

Mrs. Warren is a beautiful Black woman, and she knows it. She isn't vain, just confident. She is bold and loud, authentically herself, and she intimidates the hell out of me. His mother is happy as long as her children are, but I heard her cuss Wyant out on the phone enough times to know she could be a little overbearing and nosy. I never get the vibe that she hates or dislikes me; but if she had her pick for Wyant, it wouldn't be me. Mrs. W did not care who was in her presence when she spoke her mind. During a conversation while we were out to eat at Casa Grande, an interracial family went by our table on the way out of the restaurant. She rather loudly stated that segregation isn't necessarily wrong to have again. Everyone is free to live and love who they wanted, intermix, and be friends, but in her opinion,

"Black men should be with Black women. Period. Most white women are just using Black men to create a world of mixed babies that they love to doll up and use to perpetuate stereotypical prejudices against their own children. Ninety percent of them don't do the fucking self-work or research to be qualified to raise these Black children; they just have a form of white savior complex."

Don't even get me started on her thorough but valid rant about white families adopting Black children. By the end of her one-woman speech, hell, even I was convinced she might be right. After all, if my mother hadn't made her choices, who could I have been? Maybe Wyant deserves to be with someone of whole complexion and DNA. He shut that shit down the second I brought it up. He knew the wheels had been turning ever since she said the words, but it was the first time we had been able to be alone. I barely even thought, "Maybe your mom was right," out loud before he spoke.

"One thing about my mother is that she is fucking opinionated. I love her for it but she is not always the most situationally aware or discreet. She stands in her truth, who she is, and her beliefs. But Rue, know this: my mother's opinion is hers, and everyone has their own. I am who I am today because she allowed me the space to find and be myself. Her personal opinion on this, and most matters, is not fact and she doesn't treat it as it is. If she can see the good, she is gravy. She can still appreciate the ten percent and hold the others accountable. That is not a reflection of you, Duckie. You are here despite your mother, remember, not because of her. Find and stand in your truth."

Brain glitch avoided. He talked logical sense into me, and I could handle her truth. She isn't wrong. My mother had laid with a Black man in an act of defiance, produced a brown child and reminded that child of her regrets daily. It didn't mean my mother's ill-laced words were fact. We always hear that a child's brain is like a sponge, and it's true. As a result of my mother, and plenty of others, mine is like the abandoned sponge in a bucket full of filthy gray-black water and debris. Covered in stains and putrid bacteria. Wyant is the fresh water flowing steadily, yet slowly, into my bucket. Eventually, maybe with enough, the brownish-gray sludge inside will become a little more transparent. I'll never be fully clean, some stains will always be left on my sponge, but maybe it can be disinfected and usable once again.

Mr. Warren, Wyant's stepdad, is his wife's polar opposite but it works. He is the quiet type who prefers to sneak-watch sports on his phone and happily lets Mrs. W do all the talking. However, when he gets a few drinks down, it is fucking whiplash. He's dancing and trying to force everyone in the room to karaoke with him. He becomes friendly, open, and wants to put his arm around everyone like college buddies. Wyant is always there to be my buffer, though. If not physically creating a barrier, he is purposefully sending me to the corner store for any "missing" items we need. Or preemptively making excuses for me to retire early for the night. We compromise. I don't sneer or roll my eyes out of jealousy of his loving family, and he allows me to have a time limit for social interaction.

I feel more at peace when I'm home and can control my surroundings, interactions, and reactions. The unknown variables and forces outside our four walls take time to compartmentalize before stepping out into the world. When he proposed the vacation, my brain tried to devise every excuse not to go, but I let him speak and said nothing. I could see how excited he was and how much he missed his family and deserved this break. He wanted this trip for us. Something special. Ordinary people take vacations and enjoy the company of others, right? I am not normal, but I try for him.

Honestly, I'd be content in PJs all day with a glass of wine picking my limited, yet preferred, routine options. I am a cat lady minus the cats. Collecting books doesn't make me wake up looking like I have been in a fistfight with the dander-beast. The mere idea of this trip is triggering me. I was shit at hiding that I was irritated and insecure. I can't help but speculate that he will get sick of dealing with me and look for something, or someone, else. Someone much more agreeable.

Nervously taking a sip of my drink, my hands slip, catching the glass before it tips over; liquid still sloshes over the side, drowning everything in its path. The thin white napkin shreds and disintegrates as I wipe up the mess, mirroring how my insides are behaving. *Just breathe, for fuck's sake. What are you doing? Just pick up your shit and walk away. Stop being fucking crazy. It's not too late.* I hear her nails scratching at the door now. She's laughing at me, cackling even.

Just as I talk myself out of staying, Wyant is quickly approaching the restaurant, intently texting on the phone the entire time.

And I see that fucking smile. My smile.

FIVE
IT'S A GAMBLE

When he gave me my smile

The world came back on its axis.

It was the one time in my life,

I had hopes of no endings... disastrous.

Sweet kisses, gentle touches,

Two souls embraced,

If I were a betting (wo)man,

Thought I might win the race.

SIX
FEAR

"You deserve to be in environments that bring out the softness in you, not the survival in you."

-Ronne Brown

I KNOW FULL WELL I sound delusional right now, but I see that smile, know it just like I memorized every faded mark, scar, or faint stretchmark on his body and it's fucking mine. The first time I received my smile was about six months into our non-relationship-relationship. We weren't exclusive, even though we knew no one else existed. If you asked me our status, I'd say we were just fucking, but Wyant had slowly worked his way in and we were suddenly those hand-holding people.

We're walking like Hallmark lovers to Ruby Scoops a couple blocks up and around the corner. I peep on IG to find my favorite flavor is back; it was a gluttonous temptation that should be deemed a sin to ever take off the menu. My mouth starts to water as I remembered the last time I devoured the massive heap of purplish fresh blueberry ice cream with swirls of lemon curd and shortbread bits playing peek-a-boo throughout, all nestled on the most perfect buttery waffle cone. A symphony of flavors played on my tongue that day as the fruity, tangy, creamy, and crunchy pieces made for the perfect harmony and I wanted an encore. She creates the best unique flavors and combinations of homemade ice cream available in the 804. And yes, I am proud to say it is owned by a beautiful Black woman named, you guessed it, Miss Ruby. Full of love for her craft and her community.

A bench-table, with a tall side partition made up of a giant solid piece of wood has always been a beacon for the shop we are approaching. It's artfully done in a symbolic way with its honeycomb cutouts to match the signage. The bench seats a couple of people hanging out in enthusiastic conversation as we pass the newly opened Ms. Bee's Juice Bar. I could no longer say I wasn't a fan of veggie beverages as the Green Goddess juice was on point with her secret addition of pineapple. You couldn't go wrong with any of the fresh fruit blends, either. They have quickly become a weekly habit of mine. Wyant and I were even able to reduce his coffee addiction a bit after she opened and he started spending more time at my place. His side of the fridge is now stocked with her cold-pressed juices, bottles of his current favorite, the Grand

Rising (Renew)- a pink blend of oranges, strawberries, apples, carrots, ginger, and turmeric.

Wyant and I are mid-conversation about how great it is to see Black-owned businesses poppin' up and down Brookland Park Ave, bringing much-needed life to the previously semi abandoned strip. The only places that survived over the years are several barber shops and salons. We do not play when it comes to our hair! These two additions, along with a new burger joint and coffee shop/bbq joint, keep constant traffic. A lot of the storefronts on the strip have been freshly painted, and the sides are adorned with colorful murals depicting beauty, hope, and change. It is also July, which means it is hot enough to see the asphalt singing to the skies in the distance.

As we round the corner, regulars hanging out in the dwindling shade on the side of a colorful muraled brick building come into view. The teals, pastel pinks, sun yellows, and lime greens are a beautiful contrast to the dark brick orange. The stunning image in front of me starts to morph into gray as I slow to observe the familiar faces.

"Hey, Rue!…You cheatin' on me? You breakin' my heart, woman! I thought we were better than that!" Ronnie, a sweet, yet odd man shouts in my direction. He clearly made the ladies swoon back in the day, before his poison of choice got him in its clutches. His calloused hands clutch his heart, as he turns to walk backwards, staying in our line of vision. His eyes, still joyful after the universe had been so cruel to him, will always have that lingering sadness behind them from untold secrets and stories that were only his to tell. His body is lean, and his usually worn out, *now relatively clean, cargo pants hang from his frame. The worsening day-by-day summer heat is prevalent by his dripping face, bare chest, and sweat-drenched tee that hangs on his shoulder. He's lost a few more pounds since I ran into him last. While repulsive to some, his smile always reaches through the cage around my heart.*

I momentarily panic. Was it the 15th already? We usually make a point to meet around payday. It has been our routine for a few years now, but working from home as of recently, days are passing quickly and time is more fluid. Great, I would have to be social with more than one person at a time, and I hadn't planned on that. I did almost everything within my power to push Wyant away at this point in our relationship; seeing his non-personable, not-girlfriend being friendly with the homeless wouldn't help the credibility of the universally self-proclaimed, self published novella. Have you heard of it? It's a top selling story of self- sabotage. I can't quiiiiiite remember the name - but could be titled, "You Can Do Better Than Me." I meet Ronnie's smile with a small, closed-mouth one of my own and a fist bump. He is never offended that I don't hug him. He knows it isn't him, it's me.

"Never! How could I? We're running away together one day, right?" I reply to him in a feigned hurt voice, as we come to a stop.

His smile never leaves his eyes, but his face becomes serious as he says, "Found what you left. I shared it with the crew. We appreciate ya, lil' lady." I look at Wyant and see the wheels turning in his head. My brain decides that this is my chance to be a dick.

I lower my volume a little and whisper loudly, "Can't be talking all loud about our business Ron, but you know I got you. Only the best stuff for you." I feel the closing squeeze on my hand and the eyes staring into the back of my head, but I don't turn to answer his unspoken inquiries. "I was worried when I left it at our normal drop spot. A few eyes were around, and I've been worried about how well you can care for yourself if shit gets bad."

Somehow my potential runaway lover understands the unspoken mission and plays his part. Leaning in closer, Ronnie responds, "I been tellin' you we need a new spot. Shit's not safe out here no more, and I can't keep up with dem youngins. Could use a re-up if you can spare it. Enough to fill the bag. Lots of new people to supply since they pushed that group out of the park."

"I got you. You got the bag?" I reply. He turns around and walks back to the group of others he had been with. They exchange a few words as they hand him an almost, if not completely, empty, extra-large camping backpack. Once he made his way back, I could see one of the straps had broken. "You can't be lugging around this shit. It'll kill your back once I fill it. I'll get a new one soon."

"It empties faster than I can get it off, don't worry about me," he says and we both turn to Wyant, who at some point let go of my hand and was standing, observing. A whole mountain with the silent warning of an avalanche starting. His toned jaw and cheeks are taut, arms folded, and his beautiful umber eyes

that looked like they had flashes of gold penetrating as he observed, doing everything he could to not speak. He thought it was drugs. I knew how he felt about them. He was clear about how he had zero tolerance. "Red-lined." We agreed drugs were bad. We also agreed, while he was not as avid a partaker as me, cannabis, as he called it, was not a drug.

"I'd still like some ice cream, but I need to pop into the corner store and grab something really quick."

"What the fuck are you about to do, Rue?" I hate seeing the concern mixed with anger and disbelief in his eyes, but I am getting pissed. This is becoming a scene and not one I want a leading role in.

"Nothing that concerns you. I need you to trust me." I see the sting flash across his face but I'm not here to play games, especially not with Wyant. "Besides, you know me."

"The fuuuuuck I do. You," he points toward me, "involved me the second you started talking about it. I thought I knew you. Shit, the moment I told you my red line, you-"

I cut him off, "Look, we were having a private conversation." I am pushing buttons by not explaining further. From everything he shared with me, it's ridiculous for him to think I'd abuse that trust but I can also understand trust doesn't come easy. Drugs had been the catalyst to destroy his family when he was a child. His biological father was injured during a freak accident on the job. While he did recover physically, the addiction had already begun. Wyant's mom tried to get him into every rehab center she could but eventually, once it was clear he wasn't ready for help, she kicked him out. He continued on, out of *control until he OD'd on a bad street prescription of Oxy a few months later. Wyant, at 18, was the one to go identify his father's body. He made it clear his red-line was drugs from our first interactions. Due to his own trauma, he has a jaded view of the homeless. Not that he lacked empathy but he thought of it more so as black and white; they choose to be there or their choices put them there. His interactions with his father also played into his thoughts that most homeless were addicts of some sort.*

This is quickly becoming a test of trust. Wyant knows it as well as I do. Would my word be enough for him or would he think I would dabble with drugs after all he has been through? Two choices. Both with consequences. I glance at Ronnie, who tries to keep a straight face, before addressing my mountain man.

"Go get the ice cream. I'll meet you there, 15-20 minutes tops. You'll still be in line; it's always packed."

"I told you, if you need money, I have you, got no problem helping. I want to. You don't need to do this."

I just stare at him with gentle, pleading eyes. He is unsure if I am a little project he can fix and save. Not happening. I never relied on anyone else before or indicated to Wyant that I needed saving. I would not start now. I am the helper, not the helpee.

"Rue, we need to talk about this shi-" He points to the bag, me, and Ronnie all at once. I cut him off.

"Wyant, after I do this, you," I point to Wyant, "me," I point to myself, "and the damn ice cream can sit and talk then. I'll meet you there. Please?" I see the internal battle of conflict in him. If he goes, he would be the shit man who left a woman

31

near a street corner with shady-looking people for a drug exchange. If he stays, he risks pushing me away by not trusting in me. He is a logical person. He knows he doesn't have all the answers and doesn't want to assume.

That's who he is. The benefit of the doubt kind of guy, but the exchange of words has been clear. There were no lies said, so he wouldn't call me out. There is nothing he can do but walk away in the opposite direction, back toward his truck. He is leaving.

No man, no ice cream. This is best and deserved for him and for me. I fight the itch to turn around and instead my feet start moving me toward the corner store for my first stop. I know Ronnie will be behind me. I don't even look. I swallow hard and take a deep breath, trying to get the parade of voices in my mind telling me what to do to subside.

The ATM machine takes forever to count out the cash; $120 is all I can spare this month. I quit the bar a few weeks ago after a brawl took place and I was clocked in the head with a bottle for minding my own business. I had enough. While I made plenty, I wasn't paid enough to babysit drunk adults and play security. I had fought that fight enough. Even though I have a new decent-paying virtual job that started last week, funds were limited. I stand there counting the cash because I don't trust the machines as much as I don't trust people.

"He seems like a good one." I hear it coming from beside me. I can't look at Ronnie right now. His kind eyes will break me down.

"I know." That masculine nerdy, Star Wars and Marvel-loving man is everything I have ever wanted when I allowed myself to think happy thoughts. Soft, yet firm. Kind and assertive. Wyant sees through the bullshit and doesn't allow me to stay in my head too long. He silences the noise. Everything about my life seems to end up scorched. The odds aren't in my favor.

Wanting a chance to accept that my grasses have possibly been set aflame again, I send Ronnie off to collect items that would keep his belly happy and mouth full. I didn't need a lesson today on getting in my own way. Haven't you been keeping up? I wrote a book, remember?

SEVEN
MY SMILE: PART 1

"When people show you who they are, believe them."
-Dr. Maya Angelou

HELL'S FLASHLIGHT CAUSES ME to squint as we step outside of the corner store onto the sidewalk. I am conscious of walking slower, letting Ronnie set our pace. We walk in silence during the fifteen minute trek to the Walgreens as he eats his newly acquired food. He no longer has to ask, it is always ready for him every time we go through this routine. Honeybun first, followed by his sandwich of choice for the day. Ronnie always did that. When I inquired one time, he told me if he choked and died on his last meal, he at least wanted to go out sweet from the inside out. I got it, sorta, but I accepted it for what it was. He is all sweet. There is no sourness in Ronnie unless he has to be.

Usually, we would chat a little or he'd tell me a story that had a moral at the end. Sometimes we exchanged the most fucked up dark humor jokes we knew. Today, he senses correctly that I need a reprieve from wasted oxygen. I leave him on the little hill that separates the parking lot from the main road, opening his Coke. The sound of depleting carbonation fades as I continue through the doors of Walgreens. He is not welcome inside establishments like this. They shoo his kind away and treat them like vermin, so much for the love thy neighbor crap that most people who walk by them spew with their disingenuous tongues. Where life allows me, I try to follow commandment number one. "Love is religion."

The generic clean, yet stale odor hits my nose as I walk through the automatic doors. Instant chills spread as the cold air blasts my damp skin. The perfect cover for stroking my arms to self-soothe the unnameable feeling that creeps through me. Thirty minutes later, I am still being the indecisive bitch I always am when it comes to too many choices and Wyant comes to the forefront of my mind. He always made sure to keep tabs of my favorite meals and places. Not that I don't like trying new things. I just like routine. I could sneak little tastes off of his plate when I wanted. It keeps things simple and my head doesn't get stuck in an endless loop of this-or-that.

Going home alone after this is not something I am looking forward to. It is the pothole in the road ahead I can't see but barely have a chance of avoiding. However, I know if I can't swerve just a little, I might scrape by with only a bent wheel. Or maybe my car is so rusted at the seams that it would fall apart into pieces. Either way, there would be damage.

I blink rapidly, looking down as tears escape and land near my seemingly four feet. Wiping the sudden leaks away and looking forward, I still see two blurry sets of all the little boxes and bottles. Fucking tears are just as stupid as men. As I continue to walk slowly, my brain turns its ticket and hops on the merry-go-round of indecisiveness. How long it would take to get off, no one knows when there are fucking eight to twelve options, sometimes more, of the same damn thing for everything. Cheaper is only better sometimes but this day, it will have to do.

Time is fluid as I cruise aisle by aisle, trying to get as much as my tiny budget will allow. My small cart is almost full, as are my eyes when I realize I don't have enough for the most requested items. Inflation is a huuuge bitch. Down right fucking robbery. I am failing them just like I failed at everything else. As I switch one last thing out to replace it with two of the cheaper alternatives, the weight of the heavy hand cart I stupidly subjected myself to is being pulled away from my forearm.

Immediately stiffening and standing straight up, I turn, ready to cuss out whoever felt entitled enough to have invaded my fucking space. However, before I can get a word out, my brain glitches. I stand frozen with still balled fists as I watch Wyant pour my basket into a rolling cart that seems too full. My eyes scan the items that cradle my few measly things in comparison. Our eyes meet as I stare, confused.

"I've been following you in the store for over an hour."

Shit..Ronnie….. He's been out sitting in Hades' asscrack waiting for me. Wyant must sense where my mind went by following my glance to the front of the store.

"He's fine. He's sitting in the truck."

I follow him silently to the check-out line. I don't know how to feel. Relieved to see him. Confused that he came back to me, this is his chance at a clean break. Nervous to exchange words I knew would be coming eventually. My brain calculates the situation and the predicted outcome has too many emotions. The system is crashing. The underlying electric current building between all the chaotic feelings is not helping. It would be perfectly circuited, or we would be electrocuted to death. I am scared to find out. I am trying to save him from the fucking disaster that is me, and he just keeps coming for more. He must be more of a glutton for self-punishment than I thought.

The silent worker in front of us looks on unimpressed before I end the silent battle of war, trying to put money in his hand that keeps swatting it away. Shoving my crumpled cash toward the cashier and demanding her to take my money, she hesitantly, but with a smirk, grabs the shaking bills and I leave him standing there. The total is more than triple what I have to offer. I'm not a total bitch. I wait by the truck, ignoring Ronnie's shit-eating grin behind the slightly tinted window, to help Captain Save-a-Hoe load the never-ending bags into the truck's bed. When I jump in the back, Wyant and I lock eyes in the rearview mirror; a barrage of unspoken questions and thoughts linger between us. In that moment, his eyes show concern for his leather seats. I get carsick quickly if I sit in the back, but I'm not going to make Ronnie move. He deserves to feel like an average human, living an everyday life enjoying a regular fucking car ride and not being driven around out of pity or obligation. He deserves this moment. Plus, I probably earned this self-imposed timeout in the back with inevitable motion sickness.

Wyant realizes Ronnie would have to go far to hand out the supplies to his community so he takes charge and stops at Costco to grab some drinks and snacks in bulk. I am quiet while they yap and get to know each other. As we leave the store, I can see the shift, the softening, his views on the homeless are shifting.

We get back into the truck and Ronnie starts giving directions to deliver the food along with the hygienic and medicinal items we purchased. I am trying to be in the moment but my head is betraying me as I watch this man, my man, treat every single person we come across with such care and genuine interest. He keeps typing on his phone after walking away from a person. I know he isn't taking numbers. He is taking notes. Assessing the situation and coming up with a plan.

My prediction is correct. Not too long after, a beautiful ocean themed food truck comes around the corner, parking in the mostly empty, but littered with bodies, parking lot. I know this truck. He organized this, too. I've talked to Wyant several times about wanting to try them; The Sweet Xscape by Envy. A gorgeous, petite all around, Black woman pops her head out as she opens the side hood. Wyant walks over to speak with her for a few minutes, passes her his credit card, then turns to take a selfie at the request of the fabulous owner. Ms. Tierra starts to type on her phone, fingers moving fast as hell while simultaneously taking orders and yelling out her rules of being respectful, "We are all adults so pick up after your damn selves!"

I know, without fail, she is working out her underlying plans for her next post as she continues to type away. Updating the community and encouraging them to come out and show support as folks in the vicinity start lining up fast. She is a hot commodity in Richmond right now. Her following is loyal and ever-expanding. You have to catch her where you can as she is always on the go to the next place and trying to leave it a little better than when she entered. She has only one golden rule she always follows. If you leave the place trashed, she won't return to the location and she rightfully shames those caught littering. I knew she was strong and vivacious from watching her on the 'gram, but in person it is a vision to uphold. As she passes out her famous ice cream nachos that put her on the map, Wyant heads back to the front of the line and grabs two stacked clear containers and a cup towering with something I can't quite make out, but it looks like a drink of some sort. The gap quickly closes as he navigates the ever growing crowd of people. There is a blend of all shades and all walks of life. If I could scoop this moment and put it in a little carton, I would have a deluxe rainbow sherbet. I hear Ms. Tierra start fussing loudly. She admonishes folks jokingly, asking why all these people are lined up in front of her but no one is networking.

"Now why y'all have business cards but leave them out there in the car for? That ain't smart business and a waste of damn money. Maybe you have something of service to someone else *around you, even if just uplifting words. Network! You got all these people here, turn around and speak. No one will bite you."*

Someone cracks a joke about being teased with a good time. She just shakes her head, laughing along with the crowd. The joke lands well. A few others start taking and handing out boxes to some of the less mobile patrons. After stopping midway to offload Ronnie his personal treat, Wyant walks over plopping his deliciously drenched self on the tailgate next to me. There is space between us, too much and too little, all simultaneously. I stare back at the scene in front of us. Smiling faces, laughter, dice games, and even a small all-in-fun dissing session was going on. Music from a boombox fills the air. Our little impromptu ice cream party creates a joyous moment. I let myself bask in it and enjoy the feeling, knowing it won't last but holding on to it. The nachos are fucking delicious! I ask Wyant to try his dessert once I realize it isn't a shake after all, but rather the Biscoff Cheesecake Sundae served in a large clear cup. I almost want to trade with him. I am in heaven as the sinfully delicious, chocolate dipped waffle cone chip topped with vanilla ice cream, browned peaches, and caramel hits my tongue. I can't decide which part I like more. I glance down the street toward Ms. Ruby's entrance to see an overflow from inside to the sidewalk and down at least 50 people deep. I am not cheating on her, there is space for all the ice cream.

The sun is setting by the time we finish cleaning and jump back in his truck for the short drive back to my house. The small space was loudly void of unspoken spoken words. Instead, the faint music of the radio and the sound of the wind comes through the cracked window and fills the silence, my hand in his.

We parallel park on the street in front of my rental, my elbow propped up on the door and window simultaneously, chin tucked to fist. From the outside, you would have thought it was a family place. Probably filled with pictures of doting, in-love parents with one, two, or three children depending on the frame that catches your eye. Light yellow paneling with fresh white window trim, a fully screened-in porch, fruit trees, and bushes adorn the front area, everything neatly pruned and trimmed. It even comes complete with the little white picket fence. The only stain of the picture-perfect scene is the overgrown clover grass and dandelions. Even still, the home is in stark contrast with the neglected or abandoned homes just down either way. There are little pockets of life in this neighborhood, though, outside of the street activity in the dark. Every day there is a new fixer-upper being swiped off the market.

"Beeeeeeeeep!" A car horn and the sound of screeching tires snap me back to catch the tail end of Wyant's voice.

"Huh?" I say as my head turns, never leaving the anchor point holding up its heaviness to meet his voluptuous lips. Not his eyes. I can't look into them yet. He would try to see me. Not me, but inside of me. If I am honest with myself, looking into his eyes starts to feel like how the kids who fake-lived in my rental must have felt when walking to the outstretched arms of their parents after school. Home. Safe. Welcome. Wanted.

"The self-proclaimed dark-hearted soul has a little light after all, huh?"

He is baiting me. Caught in another lie that I can't talk myself out of. My gaze drifts from the shadow of a beard on his chin to looking forward and up, out the front window to the painted skies. The clouds are still but morphing and melding together at the same time, like they aren't quite sure which shape they want to be or what direction they want to go. I could see myself floating amongst them.

"Nope." I try to sound confident. Did I teleport to the ocean? My eyes are clouded and stinging like I have just resurfaced from the salty waves. Grateful for the glare the setting sun creates, an excuse. It makes people blink and wipe their eyes repeatedly, right?

I wait for the barrage of questions to come. Getting to the root of why I lied to Wyant before wouldn't come up. He already knew. I think back to when I told him I was nothing. I feel like the forgotten, unlabeled items tucked away in the back of the fridge. I am just rotting fruit.

EIGHT
MY SMILE: PART 2

"He stayed all winter."
-Tarryn Fisher

WHEN EVERY PERSON WHO is ever supposed to give a shit betrays, abuses, or uses you repeatedly and then leaves, how is one not indoctrinated to believe that they are disposable garbage reeking of desperation? How do you ever really trust anyone? Can I trust the man heading into the neighboring restaurant with my smile, or has he already given it to another?

Over time, I gave him as much of my backstory as I was willing to share, which wasn't much, but enough. On one of our dates, he asked me why my front yard's grass was never cut.

The dandelions were even making it hard to walk up the pathway to the front steps or backyard. When he arrived at my place, I had lost track of time and was still in my happy place. He just so happened to walk up as I tripped on some of the fucking tall yellow-topped weeds and was fussin' at them like children; they seemed out of place compared to how pristine I kept everything thing else. Surprisingly, to us both, I didn't take much time to process and think before I answered.

"No one gives a shit about dandelions. If they're lucky, they are a sore sight to the eyes from the beginning. They are immediately uprooted or trampled, doused in poison, and left to shrivel into their quick death. Then there are the unfortunate flowers that somehow fucking survive, just to become little puffballs ripped from their roots, used to blow for someone's personal entertainment, and what's left is tossed aside, zero fucks given."

I am a weed and not the kind I was craving at that moment.

"So you give a few fucks," he replies. I nod sheepishly. That is all that needs to be said. He gets it. He gets me.

When he drops me off after the date, I run. I literally get out of his truck and run into the house. I feel like new seeds have been planted inside me, and I'm scared. I had never really let myself be that vulnerable with anyone, especially a man.

I am a fuckin' coward, and I'm okay with that, I think. It's saved me countless times before. I try my best to pretend the date hadn't just happened by hanging out with my three best friends, Ben, Jerry, and this lovely lady, Canna. They listen to my self deprecation and fears. They are all I have and they take care of me as I cry myself to sleep.

The next day, a text comes through.

Wyant: You home?

I don't respond. An hour later there is a knock at the door. I open to a brown wall and step back. My eyes adjust; the wall is just a paper bag dangling from Wyant's fingers from an outstretched arm. My gaze travels from his arm to a slight strain of his biceps, bare chest, and chiseled abs, all sweat-slicked and slightly dripping. I could lick him like an ice cream cone right now. In his other hand, a thick paper cup. I don't have to look at the cardboard sleeve to know he made a stop at The Smoke Mug around the corner. He switched his regular Starbucks routine after I had made an offhanded comment about supporting small and local businesses being important to me. I don't drink caffeine but according to him, it is the shit. I also know this coffee shop is two minutes walking distance from me. What kind of idiot would run with hot coffee?

"Did you run here?" Stupid question. He is a runner. His place is a little less than three miles away. He tries to get in ten miles a week minimum and in his state of dress, it obviously pays off well. My brain blanks when he is around.

"Yes, you gonna open it?" he asks. Grabbing my hand, my arm lifts and slides under the bag's handles. The weight of my arm dropping snaps my attention from the suddenly intrusive sexual urges and the object of those desires. I turn around and head back inside, having heard the gentle closing of the door and footsteps behind me.

"Water?" I ask but don't wait for the answer as I retrieve a glass from the shelf, heading around the island to walk toward the freezer for some ice. I avoid feelings, him, the ominous paper bag, and he knows it. He intercepts my path, grabs the glass out of my hand, taking my other with his free digits, and guides me to the couch. He gently pushes my shoulders down to get my legs to cooperate with his goal. I, more or less, collapse.

He knew I was avoiding him. Gifts, compliments, or asking anyone to do anything for me leaves me uncomfortable, cringing. Still, I have been learning his love language and his projections of it and trying to lean into it a bit, for him. Again, compromise. For me, there has always been strings attached or tabs kept or simply given out of a feeling of obligation. Nothing I'm given is ever really mine or for me. It isn't my birthday or a holiday, so my brain isn't coming up with a logical solution as to why he has a gift with him. Why would he have a gift for me? What does he want from me?

My silent thoughts are interrupted. The crinkling sounds of the bag reemerge as it is placed on my lap. Wyant leans down and kisses my forehead before walking backward toward the kitchen, finger extended in my direction.

"I'll be right back. Open it." He doesn't need water; his coffee is on the coaster before me on the table. He just knows I need space for this.

I slowly pull apart the two handles and look down inside, first pulling out a duck plushie. He's called me his Duckie the last 2 weeks, but I've been scared it was not for good reason, so

I didn't ask, just went along with it. I am used to being the butt of a joke or two.

I continue to pull out two books; Dandelion Medicine by Bridgette Mars and The Dandelion Celebration by Peter Gail. Lifting the latter, I carefully balance the other on my closed knees, holding it eye level to inspect the cover more closely. It looks like old-style art on the surface of a children's book. A side-profile view of a little brown-haired girl stopping to smell a single yellow flower. My fingers slip their grip and I catch myself, but not before I see the corner of paper sticking out of the bottom of the pages. I open the cover fully, and what looks like a letter falls out, bounces off the other book and drops to the floor. Placing both books gently on the table in front of me, making sure to line them up together and with the edge of the table, I reach to retrieve the tri-folded piece of computer paper. Slowly, I open it to take in its contents. He isn't usually a man of many words, but his little notes were always heart-palpitation-inducing.

My chest is already constricting when I start to read:

Duckie,

You told me you were a dandelion.

Dandelions are good. See? Science says so, and you can't fight science.

And did you know you can eat them? Apparently, they are delectable and delicious.

I'd have to agree *wink wink*

You can see yourself as a dandelion, I can't change that, but we do not view you the same.

Dandelions may be a weed, but they are medicinal and healing when appropriately handled.

The people that blew out your puffball sent seeds to be planted in the garden of my heart. You're my dandelion now. I know they are not your cult leader's words but read and use these when your brain tells you dandelions are shit.

Stop pushing me away.

-W

Was he right? A quick flip through both books quickly tells me he is. One is dedicated to dandelion culinary dishes and other medicinal uses. It really is possibly true; dandelions had a purpose, a reason for existing outside of a delicate flower.

I can feel his presence. I don't need to look for him, my gaze moves straight to his tall frame leaning against the wall to my left. I cover my face to hide the sudden foreign feelings and words that want to surface. Wyant walks to where I am and lowers himself to his knees as I stay curled over into myself. He knows I am uncomfortable, but he assumes correctly that I want him near me. Soft, yet calloused, fingers lift my chin so we are face to face as he strokes my bottom lip with his left thumb and a rogue tear with the right. My eyes trail from his full lips to his perfectly prominent nose, up to his eyes. I hate you, Wyant Minnick.

"Why Duckie?" is all I manage to crack out through the endless questions that race through my mind. He lets out a soft laugh as he brings our foreheads together. I close my eyes again, unable to take the total weight of his intimacy. I can feel the current getting stronger. Whatever he has to say would be prolific, surely. That's who he is.

"Your eyes," he replies in a smooth tone. I pull back slightly and look at him, confused. I almost expect the response to be, "Because you are a quack!" That would have been easy. I probably would have chuckled at that. It would sting, but it was the truth. My brain can't compute the correlation between ducks and eyes, so I stay quiet and let him continue. He smirks at me, and the connection holds. I couldn't look away if I wanted to. He has trapped me again. Fucker.

"Ducks appear to float on the surface. They look serene and peaceful. Like they don't have a care in the world or fear what may lie below. Yet, they are forever aware of their surroundings. Queens and Kings on their watery thrones. Although, if you look

51

under the water, they are not floating but wading. Never stopping. That's you. All calm on the outside. To the everyday person, you have your shit together. You're the strong one. I see it in and through your eyes, though. Behind them, the wheels that never stop turning. Your brain's legs are always swimming. My Duckie." See, he is an ass. Why does he have to be so fucking good? You know what I mean?

This man saw me. All the good I try to be, the love I want but fight against, my love to give. My softness through the stoical face presented to the world. He accepts that while I try to chase the sun, I still have shadows and dance with them frequently.

"I love you," flies out before my brain can tell my mouth to shut the fuck up. I choke-cough a little and squeeze my eyes shut. If they are closed, this isn't real. Nope. Nope. Nope. Wake up bitch, we gotta go! I can't chalk it up to a nightmare.

"It, I love it!" I try to correct it, but it's too late. He hears and absorbs the words. The truth, not the lie.

I keep my eyes closed as he lifts me and repositions our bodies so he is now sitting, and I am straddling his muscular thighs. I lay my head onto his shoulder and cradle my forehead under his chin into his neck, cross my arms and tuck them between us. One of Wyant's hands runs up my back, the other cups the back of my head. A moment later, I feel myself being pulled back by the shoulders and my face cradled, bringing us inches apart. There is nowhere to run. My function buttons aren't working. No fight or flight or freeze mode to activate, but tiny little men are working overdrive to get it up and running.

"Duckie, I love you." I feel the burning in my nose rise again as he kisses one eye and the scar barely visible above my brow. "Duckie, I see you." The first sniffle escapes me. He kisses my other eye, and a small leak cracks past the barriers as his lips move to kiss the tiny scar on my chin. "Duckie, YOU are worthy." This time he gives me the gentlest kiss on my lips. I am a fucking mess. "Look at me, baby." The tiny men working to fix the issue in my body decide to take a different course of action. A convoy of new function replacement buttons is being backed in on a trailer. Acceptance. Love. Hope. Stay. In the blink of an eye, they are done and call it quits for the day.

"I love you, too." The new buttons are working.

A minute later, I take a deep breath and slowly open my eyes. I look at Wyant and for the first time, I get my smile. The kind of smile that reaches deep into your soul, almost filling every hole ever made. I unintentionally told him something that he knows, without spoken knowledge, are foreign words to my tongue. He, in return, gave me something I heard dozens of times and things my soul craved to experience but never believed existed for me, until now. He holds me close as I become a whimpering mess. His hold on me only strengthens, but he says nothing as the whimpering turns into a full blown bawling session. Can't even tell you why; maybe it was for inner little Rue feeling like she was worth a damn for the first time. Or, maybe it was because we just found our first helipad.

You know, the person who lets you just fall apart on their shoulder? They don't allow you to wallow for long, but they give you the space to just feel and, in this case, cry all your feelings *out. They know you will bounce back, just have to fall first. No need for the "stay positive," or "you got this, you're so strong." The logical side that most people's brains have. Sometimes we want to be fragile and handled with care. A safe space to land before taking off again. My Wyant is my helipad and I am his Duckie.*

It was the first night, I admitted to myself, that we didn't fuck. I didn't disassociate; I submitted fully. We stayed in sync, kiss for kiss, stroke for stroke. I slid into my priestess's DM's the next day and told her all about how her sermons and songs were making a true believer of me, that I had broken some of the chain links that were keeping my soul imprisoned.

Commandment number two, "What you wrap around your soul determines your outcome."

NINE
VOWS OF VIOLENCE (SILENCE)

Lips silenced by crossing swords.

Oxygen was minimal as the light.

The demon entered the angel's lair.

Spots of fire danced across her sight.

The nightmare had only ended.

Yet, it just began.

She makes a vow to all the fallen angels,

She'd gift them this man.

TEN
INTO THE VOID

"Smile though your heart is breaking."
-Nat King Cole

I THOUGHT MY SMILE was reserved for me, was the exclusivity I had earned the right to, like the personalized, signed books on my shelves. Mine to pull out whenever I wanted. Sole proprietorship. No one else's to claim. My tall, broad shouldered man swiftly walks through those doors and pushes a breeze carrying a particular cologne enough to share his presence even if I hadn't spotted him first. Up until recently, I thought my man was mine alone.

Family Affair blasts in the background while I sweep and do my best karaoke and signature Mary J. moves with the broom handle-mic stand. I catch Wyant from the corner of my eye, placing his phone to his ear. I head to turn down the speaker, but he motions to stop and points to the back door as he walks toward it and disappears out back. I think nothing of it and return to my one-man show and task. I finish sweeping shortly after and turn to the kitchen trash to empty the dustpan.

I am not trying to lurk, the window is right above the trash can and he is too fine to not notice and enjoy the view. He is shirtless. I am jealous of the band of his white sweats and how they hang low on his hips. I can clearly see the outline of his, well, more than average dick resting against his thigh. I want that band gone and my hands in its place. That is his spot. Running my fingers gently to caress his waist across his lower stomach to the other side could get him hard. He is my personal Haagen Dazs. Deep rich chocolate filled with sweet cream; just enough nuts to fit in your hand. The perfect treat. If I were to gently and slowly take a bite of those nuts, he would contract like he was damn near ready to come. He was also magical ice cream. Could last hours in warm environments before melting.

Wyant sits reclined on the lounge chair, his NY Giants slide-covered feet crossed in front of him. One arm flexes behind his head, his phone in the other hand, he is no longer talking to anyone as he seemingly scrolls the screen. I stand there, just taking him in his entirety. His essence, his being, his beautiful black skin and defined features, when his face changes from relaxed to a momentary mixed look of surprise and panic as he glances around and toward the house. He then lifts the phone to his ear and starts talking animatedly but his eyes are glued to the back sliding doors like he was on the lookout. I want to laugh *thinking how his expression had matched when I walked in on him watching porn a few weeks ago. His expression of a surprised toddler caught by parents after too long a silence having been up to mischievous activities. A few nights later, in a slightly drunken bravada, I had reassured him by actions rather than words; he had nothing to be ashamed of. We could probably make some serious cash if a particular password-protected video were ever to be released on OnlyFans or Pornhub. We made a reenactment of my own favorite couple to watch, LeoLulu.*

I almost want to go to him to soothe us both, but the feeling leaves as quickly as it appears. The more he talks, the more his face softens. Whatever the person was saying to him was causing him to laugh and smile wide and warmly. I don't like this. I want to run to him and steal his attention and have those looks and sounds pointed at me, but I feel like an outsider; my presence is not welcome. Voices ping back and forth in my mind like two friends gossiping about the latest episode of "Rue's Life"....

"Who the fuck is he talking to?"

"Maybe it's his sister?"

"Naww bitch, he don't look like that when it's his sister."

"Maybe it's a friend?"

"A friend he's fucking!"

"What if…"

"What if nothing! He is playing her ass, and the dumb bitc—…."

I throw the dustpan down frustratingly, telling my mental narrators to shut the fuck up as I turn away before I could see anymore, abandoning my fun; my cleaning mood is officially fucked, with a headache forming on top of it. I collect my tray filled with my natural preference over pills, sit on the couch and think of how I want to approach this as my fingers angrily push the sticky green leaf into the black-stained chamber, flicking the lighter and inhaling. I hold it in as long as I can. By the time Wyant walks back in the house, I am sprawled out on the couch, arm across my face letting Zhavia's voice soothe me into submission. I am not quite there yet. He kisses me on the forehead on his way out of the room. The word shower is the only word he spoke to register, but it is the only one needed.

Five minutes later, I am staring at his iPhone. According to the call log, there has not been a sent or received call since earlier this morning. Wyant should know better than that. Checking his background apps (mentally keeping track of which order they were opened, of course), I pull up his calendar, his most recent entry still open to a date five days away. No typical label like, "lunch with so and so," or, "meeting with....," that usually accompanies his planned encounters. Just an initial, "K," a place and a time. Looks like we both had somewhere to be that day. I have to stay calm and collected; my inner Bernadine Harris is ready, legendary fire starter kit in arms, and holding a look that conveys, "I got you Sis, just say the word."

Later that evening, I pick a fight when he comments how sexy an actress is on the tv. He pulls me in and holds me close. His deep inhale bridges any gap that remains between our bodies and I want to embrace the warmth that envelops me.

"I love you, but you confuse the hell out of me sometimes, woman."

On any given day, it was me pointing out sexy actresses to him or pointing out nice curves, legs, smiles, hair, or whatever caught my eye. I am the most unmaterialistic person, yet the most emotionally expensive woman one can be with. My emotional needs change like the wind at times. My love language is a blurry mix of all the choices and it takes more than many are capable of to keep up, let alone want to continue a relationship. I imagine a relationship with me is an endless game of The Floor is Lava. Each round you are given different pathways and all the pieces to the puzzle or items needed to make it to the other side safely. At times you have to double around and try another avenue, but once you make it across, you win and are safe - at least for that round. I can't even handle a "me." If I smell weakness I pounce, yet that is just what I am at my core; weak. Could he see through it all? Had my weaknesses laid him down in another woman's bed? In "K's" bed?

I refuse to give him the satisfaction of telling him he's right so I move to slightly nudge myself away. He tightens his grip. He won't let my inner commentary keep me from hearing his words, his deep voice silences everything.

"I don't know what's gotten into you today, baby, but you think I don't have my insecurities? My own flaws and shit I'm still working on? I have fucking plenty. You are beautiful and I internally battle with appreciating when you are glanced at and wanting to rage on a fucker's face for even thinking to look at you. At the end of the day I'm glad I've bled, cried, and been scarred over the years so now I am able to smile, laugh, and love with all my heart's desire with you."

For the moment, everything in my mind disappears and my love for Wyant takes over any other emotion as his lips leave a random, slightly damp, trail across my neck and back. I feel the hem of my long shirt as it glides up my body and settles at my hips. When he slides his hand over my thigh to lift my leg, I don't even put up a fight. He settles his hardness between my folds and drops my leg. As kisses become little suckles and nibbles, his hand entangles my curls in his fist, guiding my head further back to expose my neck. His tongue traces the side from the bottom up until his teeth bite into the soft flesh below my ear as his other hand squeezes my breast, taking the small brown bud at the end between his fingers, pinching almost until the point of pain. My body arches farther back into him, craving more of what he is offering. One palm against the headboard and the other gripping the side of the bed, I start to rock and rotate my hips, stick my ass farther into him, creating the perfect angle where his shaft starts to rub my clit just the right way. The slickened friction causes me to feel myself start to soften and coat him with my wetness as his hands and mouth continue to cater to wherever they can reach. As I feel a slow warming start to build, my hand goes between my legs to guide him, wanting him inside of me now. Before I could even get past slipping in the tip, he pulls away from me.

"Come back!" I whine.

My shirt is up over my head before I can even comprehend what is going on and the next blink has me staring at the ceiling. I shiver as I feel the goosebumps take over my skin. I know what he is doing, and I don't want fucking mind games tonight.......

but I just lay there. He should be fucking me right now, not trying to love me or heal me.

"If you want it, you have to let me in. Let me see you, Rue."

This is always his test for me when he feels I seem off somehow or stuck in my head. I can let him fuck me any nasty way you can imagine but to lay bare and spread myself for him to canvas as I pleasure my body, still was something I did with hesitation. It means to submit fully, to be vulnerable in a way that is deeper than having his tongue in my ass. It means the focus is on me, solely me and my pleasure is in my own hands. It is my choice.

I close my eyes and breathe deep as I slowly bend my knees and let them fall out to the sides. Muscles all over twitch slightly as a portion of my brain fights the urge to move and cover myself. There is an unspoken way in which Wyant has managed to silence my inner sexual complexity through our time together. In the beginning, when it's fresh and new, it's easy to be caught up, focused on the moment and be able to silence the inner monologue, but with time and more familiarity, the more I lose my spark, the less present I become. Wyant is the first one to not settle for a present body and absent mind. He is greedy and wants it all. Like the stupid-bitch I am, I fall for it hook, line, and sinker.

I push and he calls my bluff, refusing my advances until I agree to let him take control. No one controls me. Hell, even I can't control me, but over time I see he doesn't want to obtain total control, or overly dominate; he wants me. Unspoken rules have been created over time between us that I didn't even know I needed.

"Eyes, Rue."

He is always close by, but not close enough. Too far away and I can almost forget he is there, too close and he knows I will play dirty to get the focus off of me. I was only able to outsmart him a handful of times before he caught on that blow jobs are the perfect way to make him cave. The last time I tried, he flipped the game and kept me going. Fucker made sure he remained right outside of my reach other than my fingers being able to graze the tip of his dick and spread the precum that glistened on the tip of the bulbous head. And so I let go and let him win. Am I losing me in the process?

I sit in front of the fire pit, my right thumbnail wedged in the middle grooves between the top and bottom front teeth while the other hand holds a wasting-away-cigarette. Compromise, or some shit I had learned in actual therapy, comes out of the depths of my brain and decides to make an appearance. My therapist would probably be proud that her ramblings somehow stuck as I would intentionally detach when she started going in too deep. Dissociative and adjustment disorder is a bitch, but she's my bitch, best friends forever. Functioning depression is my bestie's little sister that I can't get rid of, so I have no choice but to let her stay. Sometimes she behaves but most of the time, she's just a pain in the ass. My eyes move to the end where the inch long ash is starting to bend until it breaks off sending speckles of ash out into the wind as the bulk hits the ground and breaks apart. I watch as it rolls and hits a blade of grass. It disintegrates and is no more. Like it never existed. Maybe the ashes were on to something...

A few moments after entering, he is led to one of the tables. Of course, it's the one in front of the damn potted trees, leaving me with limited glimpses. His back is to me, but I can see him settle in the seat, now a little hunched over the table; the slight movements tell me he must be doing something on his phone or messing with something on the table. My trance is broken by a beautiful young woman walking like a bitch in heat on a mission to claim her prize. The banging in my ears is getting even louder, and as the red starts to fade, my breath halts when I see *her* face as she takes off the sunglasses. Her features are similar to my mother's when I was a child. Fucking tree. The fake shrubs are blocking my view more than giving me access. I only get a peek, but my anger sits at a simmer that this whore makes me think of another foul woman in my life. The bile rising in my throat is as sour as the rotten milk that is half of my DNA. People like her live to latch on like fucking parasitic wasps, infecting the host without its knowledge or permission and garnering control over the mind and body. These wasps are vile and unforgiving. They should all be eradicated.

The wind blows in my favor and I see Wyant stand and embrace her; that's not odd. It's the vibe of familiarity that throws me. I let go of my glass and grab my knee, squeezing to feel something real to keep me grounded. Too scared I would break it if I keep it in my hands, or maybe I would chuck this shit in the direction of their heads. I inhale deeply and cut my eyes as I see her choose the seat next to my man instead of across. Now they seem to be in an animated conversation, she constantly leans into him when she laughs or says something. *Sneaky bitch. I see you.* The door's wooden panels are now cracking under the beating they are taking. The she-devil is finding her way out, one way or another. There is no escape.

I look away when he side-hugs her and pulls her in for what seems like a kiss. I can't watch anymore. I'm pretty sure anyone who sees me right now would think I'm an addict by the way my body is shaking and twitching, fighting everything in me to stay rooted in place, grounded in the waning light.

How could he do this to me? With HER? Of all the FUCKING people on this planet! He's seen photos of the monster that raised me. The universe is cackling at me as I take in version 2.0 of my mother.

As the internal rage intensifies, the pressure builds steadily; the door gives way under sheer force as she is standing there, hand stretched, ready to play tag but wants to be "it." The blurry silhouettes don't know what to make of the dissevering happening in the corner, but none of the swirling figures approach or say a thing. I cower into the bench, folding my head in my hands, rocking back and forth. My bouncing knees cause the clattering symphony of silverware, cups, and dispensers gently tinkering to sound like pots and pans being used as symbols next to my head.

I don't know what to believe anymore. I used to believe in God but now we see other people, even though He is still my side man. We often bicker one-sided, me telling Him all the things I think need to be better. Cursing Him for misfortunes but thanking Him for the little things. I have been holding onto Him, unable to let go. I am scared He isn't real, but then, what if He is real? It all seems like a fucking lie. Same way I was led to believe the love I gave in life freely would return to me.

Too many sounds.

Too many eyes.

No outstretched hands.

Not enough oxygen.

I'm that little girl who is less than nothing. Invisible. Disposable. *Mommy!! Help me! ANYONE!*

The door bursts into a hundred different pieces.........

Everything is amiss in the abyss.

Sunshine is only an eclipse.

Silent yet clamorous.

Docile to dangerous.

Darkness.

Void of light.

_____.

ELEVEN
SPECKLED PEBBLE

Mother Earth shifted; did anyone else feel it?

Blinking could have caused you to miss it.

Vacant, but she is overflowing.

Down

Down

Down

Splash....or maybe it was splat.

Too much, too fast.

The current rapidly churned, mixing all that red she
was pouring.

Nothing resurfaces, a nature's mystery again occurring.

Blue and white.

Mother Earth is no longer showing signs of her anger.

A pocketed speckled stained pebble to remember.

Only after I crushed the weighted stone.

Did I spark a pre-lit cone.

Perfect day for a hike.....

TWELVE
TUNNEL VISION

"The devil asked me how I knew my way
around the halls of hell.
I told him I did not need a map
for the darkness I know so well."

- t.m.t.

WAS IT SUPPOSED TO rain today? My face feels like hot asphalt sizzling in release as cool misty rain falls upon it, snapping my attention back to the real world. *Where am I?* As I spot the sign, I am not shocked to see I'm on the trails near Byrd Park. My subconscious led me toward one of my safe havens, not too far away. One of the few places I regularly visit, The Poe Museum. He is one of my favorite poets. It was like the universe aligned for me, for once, when I chose Virginia as my new settling grounds. A quick Google search of the many theaters and museums in the city sold me on Richmond to call base.

Continuing forward, I turn my face up with squinted eyes to the wet pastel sherbet-streaked sky in the distance but void of color above me, which tells me that I must have been walking around for a few hours now. The comprehensive berth people give me as they walk past suggests I must look disheveled or sinister. A smirk settles on my face, they have nothing to fear, yet they should be scared; wounded creatures will strike first. I barely managed to talk my way out of the coffee shop clusterfuck after the waitress approached me. I muttered a quick explanation of news about an unexpected death as an excuse for my bizarre behavior, letting my feet guide me unconsciously as I got lost in my head to get my shit together enough to function correctly. I am ready to face him. To face her. They don't deserve me, but they earned everything they would get from me. Play stupid games, win stupid prizes, and I am fresh out of fucks to give out. There is one last game for the grand prize, and we would all win or lose - together.

bbbbbbbbrrrrrrp....bbbbbrrrrrrrpppp.

I hear more than feel the muffled vibrations of my phone going off.

WYANT CALLING......

"Hello?"

"What's up, babe?" I'm proud of how normal my voice sounds.

"Duckie, you okay? I texted you a few times. Came home from work to grab my gym bag. Your car is here, and you aren't. I was worried." Work huh… this muthafucker thinks I was born yesterday.

"Yeah, I'm fine. Finished my stuff early today and wanted to walk downtown by the river to read a bit. I took an Uber, so I didn't have to worry about finding parking." Semi-believable since parking downtown is a nightmare. "Sorry, I should have left a note or texted you. I didn't think I'd be gone this long." He hesitates before responding. This isn't like me. I always remember to update him on my whereabouts. He is a worrier. Or so I have been manipulated into believing. Must be so he can keep tabs for selfish reasons.

"I have plans with some of the guys to play ball for an hour, but I can cancel. I'll come and scoop you up instead." I pull up my maps app. Shit..... I'm at least a 30-35 minute walk from where I should be, not the 10 minutes it would take him to drive.

"I was thinking about cooking for dinner. I still need to go to the store. You go ahead and meet the guys. I'll Uber to the fresh market by the house and walk home from there."

"You sure? I don't mind coming to get you and ordering something. There is a new episode of Mandalorian out." Mhm.

"Of course! I'm actually enjoying the fresh air and misty weather today. I'm turning into you with your Pluviophile disorder, but it's actually passed over. Any special requests?"

"Mmmmmm, how about stuffed shells for dinner and you for dessert?" His sexual vibe is doing nothing for me. The mere continuing sound of his voice is causing my veiled anger to start pushing its way front and center, my sarcasm fitting.

"You'll be the death of me."

"Death by orgasms sounds like a fun way to go." Wyant's voice barely registers.

"If only we could choose our fate. I'll see you soon," I reply.

"Love you Duckie, be s-" I end the call before he finishes. I'll pass it off as an accident if need be.

The Uber driver turns the music up with his focus on the road. Trevor... Travis, or whatever the hell his name is, catches wind of my "Do Not Disturb" vibes after attempting small talk and getting little to no response. Thirty minutes later, I'm standing outside the little market. I enter and make a straight shot for the bathroom. The dull fluorescent lighting isn't my friend, but no ring light could fix this shit. The semi-contained top bun has fluffed in size, random curls shooting all over the place, and my slicked-back hair and edges have curled, making me look like a drowning Chia Pet.

I chuckle in disbelief as I never leave the house looking less than "neat," if only my mother could see me now..... *Shit.* My hair gets stuck in the elastic tie as I try to undo the fucking disaster on top of my head. The more I try to untangle and free my hair, the more frizzy it becomes and causes the tie to constrict tighter.

"God already cursed me with you, Rue! He could have at least given you fucking good hair instead of this unmanageable shit."

I blink back my tears at the sudden memory.

My name is indicative of my origin. I had been told from birth I ruined her life. She always made sure it was a constant reminder. My head is yanked back as the thin comb, not meant for my hair texture or type, gets tangled in a mess of knots.

"Owwwwww!!!"

"Aghhhhhhh, I can't deal with your shit anymore. I got something for you! I'm getting rid of this problem TODAY!!!" *The comb is yanked repeatedly as stinging tears fall from my face.*

"No, please don't. I'll take better care of it!!! I'll learn!!!" I *cry as my body recoils with each pull. My echoes of pain only ignite her fury more.*

My scalp is on fire as I am pulled to the kitchen. I am dragged by my hair wrapped in my mother's engulfed fist. My struggles only cause her grip to clamp tighter and tighter as I hear the wooden drawers slamming one by one. The jingles and clanks of their disturbed contents create a rhythm that sends my brain spiraling, and my gut feels what the other organ has not yet processed; it didn't have all the information. What is she looking for???

With force unbeknownst to my frail 90-pound body, I kick and claw my way free. I spin and stare across from me. The most demonic yet beautiful version of Edward Scissorhands stares back. She is holding the side of her face, but my eyes zero in on the blades that seem to have replaced her right hand.

"You little fucking bitch!!!!!" my mother screeches. As she lunges for me, I take the chance to bypass her, running for the hallway. I can almost see around the corner.

Did I fall??

Why is the corner of the wall coming toward me so fast??? CRACK!

What happened!?!?

Specs of glitter dance across my vision as I am ripped back again. The hand death-gripping the back of my neck takes most of the weight as my legs try to give out, but I am placed right back up just as fast.

She's not done.

I went too far. I disobeyed Mother, which meant I disobeyed Him.

Her other hand clutches my roots, gripping with all her might as she forces my wobbling body forward. My brain is swimming as we stand in front of the wall with old family photos full of happiness and fun times. The common denominator is that they are all void of me. I beg God to take me; I don't want this anymore. The spaces between the mismatched frames are filled with different kinds of white Jesuses, and I am losing the staring contest with white Jesus in "meh" pose. Ha! Fitting, given the circumstances. He shows me through visual cues, "What do you want me to do about it?"

I hear Mother spewing behind me, but I am transfixed on the face before me.

Mother always told me he was a white man after I had blabbed that the cute Black boy at school told me his granny said to him that Jesus wasn't white but a little darker than me. After a while, and enough lashings to pay for my sins of blasphemy, Jesus became white Jesus in my mind but nameless in my heart.

I clench my eyes as hard as I can as white Jesus comes in for fast kisses.

So much pain before the numbness and darkness settle in. I remember my last thought being for white Jesus to answer my unspoken but on-repeat prayer. It comes from my favorite movie (only sneakily watched while Mother was out), Forrest Gump.

"Dear God, make me a bird so I can fly far, far away from here," with my addition of, "or let me sleep forever."

I don't know what all happened when I was unconscious. The pain in my body barely registers before I notice all the clumps of curls around me, and Mother is nowhere in sight. The clock on the microwave says 7:42 PM. It is Wednesday; she is at bible study and will be back soon. I have less than an hour until her return, but I don't want a round two. I know the routine.

Clean the mess.

Make myself scarce.

Don't even breathe too fucking loud. You don't exist!

Weeks later, once my always too-tan skin is blemish free and the scabs have healed, Mother sits back and sees her most recent arts and crafts project isn't to her liking. It only goes downhill from here; dragging me into a beauty store and asking a white lady what she could buy and do to fix the mess "I" made of my hair seems like a logical solution.

The lady looks at me, scrunching her nose, shaking her head in disappointment. Mother plays the doting maternal figure wanting to help her disturbed child. She did this next art project herself, of course, and I fucking hate it. After it dries, it is frizzy and uneven. I am Angelica's Cynthia doll. Once it is cut to be even, I look more like Bozo the Clown. My only saving grace is that it is juuuuust long enough to put into a ponytail to cover the bald spots.

For years, I never rebelled with my hair again. Lessons learned. But now, I feel a need brewing deep.

BANG...BANG...BANG!!

"You alive in there?!?!" Someone beating on the bathroom door rips me from my thoughts. I momentarily forget where I am until I focus and look around, settling on the fucking mess staring back at me.

"Just a minute!" I yell at whoever is on the other side. I give up trying to fix the damage and rummage through my bag for another hair tie. I gather my hair as best I can, refasten a disheveled top bun, and swing the door open to face an 8.5x11 piece of paper. She has a serious case of the crinkles, probably from the disgusted expression that seems to be permanently stamped on her ordinary face. I almost want to apologize, but her turned-up face and accusatory eyes switch my empathy to, "Fuck you!" Can't a woman have a fucking breakdown in peace? I opt to say nothing more as I pass by her, slightly shoulder-checking on my way out.

The grunts and muffled insults cut off when the door slams shut behind her. Sick and tired of people and their fucking bullshit. On the one hand, she should have moved and given me more space. On the other hand, I just wanted to do it. I violated someone else for simply an upturned nose, yet would strike at anyone who dared to invade my space. We are all hypocrites. Grabbing an arm basket, I start walking toward the aisles with ingredients not already provided by the garden at home. Fresh, canned, or dried fruits, herbs, and veggies are not of scarcity in my kitchen. I usually keep myself stocked for the week this time of year. I fear being limited or starved, as before.

My sanity is an ever-growing war reaching its peak with itself, but one side has a feared leader. It is becoming more robust with each passing minute. Once I collect everything needed to complete my stuffed shells and sauce dinner, I pause and impulsively grab a pack of thick-cut bacon. My conscious mind faintly acknowledges I am a little triggered when it realizes I would eat this raw, but it doesn't care.

The blinking green lights on the microwave read 12:15 AM. I am starving; the now empty plate of Mother's once-a-day allowed meal consisting of her hours-old, leftover, overly mayo-ed bologna sandwich had been scarfed down by me hours ago. Normally, it is enough after I drink a few glasses of water but tonight, no amount would quench my hunger pains. I tip-toe into the kitchen, sure to miss any squeaks that would make my presence known. I quietly open the fridge door, searching for my irregular snack, but one of the most preferred treats. The plastic Ziplock bag unzips with no sound. The hum of the fridge masks my thievery. The plan for tonight is to steal just one or two pieces; not enough for Mother to notice anything is missing from the giant bag of uncooked bacon. I know I have gone too far by piece four, but I can't stop myself. After six pieces, tears fall as I place the off-limit item back in place. Just maybe she would be in a drunken haze and not remember.

Who am I kidding? Sober or boozed out, I am always to blame. That night was the last time I ate bacon for almost ten years. I made it two days before "Thou shall not steal" was etched in my mind and welted on my back.

I had finally let myself believe in...in something. That something was everything. He was everything. As I walk home, a smile spreads across my face. This will be the last time anyone fucks with me, but this smile is what Wyant processes as joy for him as I walk in the door. I don't correct his false sense. I want to enjoy these final moments before it's time to enter the arena.

Always hold on to something; without something, nothing is left. When there is nothing, there is space for everything. Even the shit you have been caging away- purposely lost, forgotten. Some things never need to be released. Curses are often locked away, hidden in or on an object. Safely put away in a mix of unmarked boxes. Do you really want to take that gamble? I thought I wanted to. I should have just left it all packed away and been a loner with a tiny home and tiny homestead in the middle of some creepy woods. The perfect balance of light and dark for someone like me.

THIRTEEN
QUESTIONS & ANSWERS

— — — — — — , where are thee??

I made you leave and never come back??

Did you exist before? Who were you before there was me?

My existence depended on you!!

Do YOU not understand??

I need to show you again?

Twice and in-between

Do you see it, the end?

Shade of a different kind, anything else, may there have been a chance?.?.

Amongst the flames lie answers?

At the ready-battle stance.....

FOURTEEN
UNHINGED

"I became insane, with long intervals of horrible sanity."
-Edgar Allen Poe

RUN...RUN...RUN! WYANNNNNNT!

My screams echo and dissipate into the dark.

My eyes fly open to see the fan above me in the dim room.

It's been years since I have felt this unsettled. I should just take my sleeping pills, but I hate them; barely like to take a damn Tylenol when I have a fever or something. I zone in on the clock to my left - 4:20 AM reads back. A lifeless internal laugh happens when my brain registers the time and irony of what my mind wants right at this moment. While my body also craves being in a comatose state, it's too late. What little sleep

I get now is filled with not only dreams but more nightmares of one's realities.

I look around, momentarily panicking. Everything feels wrong and out of place. I reach for Wyant, his usual space next to me is empty and untouched. After a minute, my brain recognizes I'm in the guest bedroom. It feels foreign. I've never slept in here before. My breathing is still hard as I focus on one blade of a slow whirring fan above me. Watching it spin for a few moments to try to center myself. I don't usually get out of bed at night once I am down for the count. The insomnia cycle has evaded me this last year. Throwing the covers back, my skin instantly riddles with goosebumps. Standing from the bed, the deep rust-colored mumu sticks to my back and legs. I don't want to leave the room, but according to my throat, I just ran a 5k and need hydration. Peeling the soggy fabric from my body and opting for a new t-shirt, I grab the sweats on the floor and clumsily throw them on before heading to the kitchen. The slight click of the unlocking door causes me to feel anxious. A trailer of my nightmare still plays in the background of my mind.

Fucking hell....Bright-ass LEDs temporarily blind me as I squint, rapidly blinking, reaching in to grab the bottle of water from the shelf. I use my foot to close the door, leaving behind a blueish-black hazed kitchen. The winded air and moonlight casts shadows that dance as if they are calling me to join them, and I want to. It's less scary out there than the nightmare in here at the moment. Leaning back to drain the bottle so fast that I feel a burning bubble in my chest, but I still need more. I haven't eaten much the past few days and water is helping to make my stomach stop tying in knots. I check the fridge for another one and come up empty. The only thing in there to drink is a few beers I can't stand the taste or smell of and a bottle of reisling. I pull that out and place it on the counter for later. This could be my dessert. My fridge is looking scarcer as the days pass.

With no water in sight, I close the door and enter a staring contest with the sink. I don't drink tap water; it's disgusting. I'm also picky about my brand of bottled water. Some taste weird, some too minerally, and others have just enough thick viscosity to make me gag. I need to make an exception but won't be happy about it. Reaching for my large custom-made tumbler out of the cabinet, the shortest smile comes and goes; it's my favorite. A member of our self-appointed cult, *Passionate Little Nutcases,* for Father Fisher made it. I had been searching for a new tumbler resembling me and had come up flat. Remembering my fellow *PLN*'s beautiful designs led me to reach out and see if we could collab. She did it justice. She did *me* justice. She even had me in my preferred comfy clothes. A literal character of me sitting cross-legged in panda-covered

PJ bottoms and a t-shirt. She is holding an open book up, covering the lower half of her face. Of course, the book is one of my faves written by the mighty priestess herself. *Marrow.* The other side is adorned with some of my favorite commandments. I don't bring myself to admire it like I usually do. It's like she and they are here with me, and I'm ashamed. The lost disciple. I want her presence close to me in some way. I opt for the chipped short glass next to it. As the water fills, I'm staring out the window lost in rapid thoughts. Coldness running down my hand surprises me; the glass slips from my hand and settles in the drain hole. Water starts to fill the sink. I am that glass, wedged in and drowning.......

"Awake....So thirsty.

Walk....Quenched, stumbled back to bed in a long tee.

Dream....In a place where one wasn't lesser.

Flutter....What is that pressure?

Awake....On top he mounted.

Pain....What he possessed this time was five finger discounted.

Silence....Dare not again close my eyes.

FUCK HER...She knows yet she only chides."

"SHIIIT!!!!!" Picking up the glass, I throw it aimlessly away from me. Water escapes onto my face and in my eyes during the hurl but I hear the glass make contact with something, CRASH!, followed by a thud. Using the t-shirt to wipe my eyes, I head over and turn the light on to see my damage. Scanning the room until I see my invisible target practice results. My current art project, a stack of poems I have been writing through the week, lies unscathed on the living room table. Only a few droplets of water have hit the pages, the damp spots waving under the moisture making their presence known. Moving closer, I see the colorful little box lying on the floor, its truths spilling out for the world to see and surrounded by shards of glass. Watching as a few moon-kissed pieces float around, looking for somewhere to settle. My glance moves to the shelves that line both sides of the entertainment system. The lack of light makes most of the overflowing spaces look like censor markers against the slightly glowing walls. My collection is vast and expansive, yet primarily untouched. The few books that became my survival guides are the only pages frequented and where they lie, the moonlight is a beacon to come to them. One that I ignore. I close the gap slowly, taking in each item scattered around my feet. Bending to pick up each one with delicate yet shaking fingers to place each piece of my soul back into the tiny box. The lid won't stay closed now; things aren't fitting back into place like they should. The hinge breaks under the pressure of my force.

What happens in the dark always comes to light, and often, we strike our own match...

FIFTEEN
LOCS OF THE PAST

No more fresh starts.

Who is she to be now?

Each crown adorns a new do'

She could be her,

She could be you.

Colors were running limited,

She only had one left to choose.

Red like the flames she deserved to live in.

But the shade that had used her as a muse.

Chopped little bundles of rainbow colors,

The last thing I ever wanted,

Was to become my mother.

SIXTEEN
CHURCH OF THE PEOPLE

"Your intellect may be confused, but your emotions will
never lie to you."
- Roger Ebert

TOO MANY OPTIONS MAKE me anxious, but I want the
possibilities; everything must be perfect. Almost done
but it is draining, running around all day. People either
suck the energy right out of me or I absorb all of theirs.
Both are exhausting and I am fucking ready to get this
over with. My final stop has me at good old Wally
World, and as I turn down the aisle to search for the
last two items on my list, I delete them from my notes
and put my phone back in my pocket. The damn wheel
of the cart gets stuck. Maneuvering to get back
correctly, I look up, catching sight of a group of four

older teens huddling close while engaging in conversation about whatever has their attention on the blonde's phone. I focus on the girl at the end. While participating in the discussion, she's not as engaged, her body language signaling "uncomfortable" with her arms crossed under her chest like she's protecting herself and her laugh is not quite the same as the others. No one around her could tell, but I could. She doesn't fit in.

A voice in my head starts to beg, feeling the twinge to simply belong while missing a genuine connection with someone....anyone, maybe her but I block it out. There is no need for "woe is me." I am no better than those who have transgressed against me. We are one and the same, destined to the same outcome, at least we will be. I may end up alone, but it won't be for lack of company. I forge ahead full stride to the end, stopping when the 3-foot wide, 4-foot high shelf of scarcely stocked products comes into view.

It doesn't need a label; it's glaringly visible because it's nearly invisible. Looking up and down the shelves, my eyes quickly land on the bigger boxes....Bingo....it isn't hard. There are only a few. I take the yellow box with red and green lines that brings memories of burning follicles, fried edges, and many tears to the forefront. Tossing the box in the basket, the smiling face on the front no longer visible; I didn't want to feel shame. I can hear her in my mind, mocking me, telling me I am a fool.

I gaze at the predictable display in the personal care aisle I have come to. My eyes shift to the left, where I delicately start running my fingers down the seemingly infinite sea of colorless visages with matching expressions. The blatant preferential treatment and society's biases are painfully evident. I make my way down to my limited array of options, only slightly optimistic that one of them will fit my needs. At least here, I still have access and don't have to be embarrassed to find an attendant to open a locked cover while uncomfortably hovering to keep track of how many items I take. One of these should do. Picking up one in each hand, my palms start to sweat; I need to make the right choice. And should have brought the picture with me. A mental face I have seen all my life is suddenly fuzzy and out of focus, colors all blurring together. I can't quite make it out, but it's enough to know neither will do. Spinning the cart around to surf the rest of the aisle, my irritation is growing. My usual resting bitch face wouldn't be; it feels active. These brands don't hold color to my hair, but I won't need a touch-up. Scanning continues until I glance up to a higher shelf and finally see who I'm looking for staring back at me. Persephone amongst the Poison Ivys. She always finds me. I don't know whether to hug the box close to me or destroy it, but I settle for throwing it into the cart with my other items. Time to get the hell out of here.

Attempting to cut through the clothing section, navigating my basket through a minefield of strollers, baskets, and bodies belonging to one "cool mom" group is inevitable. They see me, pretend they don't, or think I'm not worth moving their shit out of the way for. So I resist the urge to play bumper cars with their shit and methodically make my way through. *Bitches.*

Just mosey around aimlessly aisle after aisle? Nope. Doing it in forced interactions with those in company? Fuck that, too. Circumstances causing me to live life for years as a lone drifter before settling in Richmond left me content being alone but open to meeting someone eventually. Wanting to give normalcy a try one last time, but I should have known better. Wyant is Willy Wonka to my Charlie; he let me see all the candy my little heart could want, sample a few pieces with the promise it could all be mine. Only I won't get my happy ending. He strung me along only to rip the golden ticket in my face when it's time to pay up. Now it is solely me because when you enter a relationship with someone and they alone are your main circle of support, who do you have when they're gone?

His people are just that, his to begin with and never mine. I won't be the one missed or that tears are shed for. I'm tossed in the bottom of the bin and absent from their minds, time and time again. No one has proven me wrong. I admit it is partially my own fault. If I put in a little more effort with people in general, then maybe I could have a tribe of my own to fall back on by now. Who am I kidding? Even the *PLN*s would shun someone like me. They are good trouble and I am simply bad all around.

During a private confession once, Father told me I was a blue light wrapped in chains. That I was good and deserved good things. I don't know if she was right, but she is light. The North Star that leads me while climbing out of the darkness - every time, so she has to be. Lately, current thoughts are filled with a peasant seeking answers to my coveted question, "Is it Father who is blinded by Her faith in me? Is She a false prophet sent here to gas me all up for it to all burn down anyway?"

Maybe I'm not a blue light. At this point, I pretty much know I'm not. I am a green light. Toxic, poison green light wrapped in chains for a reason. What's the only color left when everything decays away? That's probably the most fitting. Black, like my soul.

Assimilation for those who lie within the parameters of certain hues, like me, has been necessary and ingrained to become an unconscious act for as far back as I can remember. I need to be more, or less, to fit in here or there. However, I am deemed worthy of a temporary seat at their table if I try hard enough, feign interest in their lives, speak like them, and dress like them. Fake it until you make it, right? Countless outings where I find myself within a particular group doing pointless shit such as fucking Target runs cross my mind. I hate Target. That fucking place steals my money everytime and the people who frequent often suck and are stuck-up. Walking around with those delicious but overpriced decaf Caramel Frappes, green teas and shit. I can do it, though - messy top buns, yoga pants, and t-shirts. I am the master of code-switching, but I'm fucking tired.

That's why I chose Walmart today, the church of the people. Come as you are, no matter how fucked up or put together you aren't. I can wear his baggy sweats, my black and white letterman jacket, black combat boots, a hat stitched with the same initials of my "church" adorning my back and thick-rimmed black shades. Most won't bat an eye. There are plenty of folks to look at and gossip about. Walmart is like a worldwide fashion show on acid. You never know what colorful trip is around the corner. I look "red carpet" compared to several I pass today.

Head slightly nodding to the beat while being serenaded by SZA's sexy voice in one of my ears, I dig into my bag, full of too much shit, looking for my wallet to prepare for check out, slightly panicking even though there are at least two full baskets ahead of me. While I may look the part of a tough bitch, nothing will make my ears turn red and accumulate boob, brow, and vag sweat faster than being an inconvenience to the person behind me. People can be assholes; me, I'm that asshole. At least mentally. I often catch myself being personally irritated when the situation is reversed and biting my tongue. As I said before, hypocrite.

Looking across the checkout at the candy bars has me noticing the couple ahead, standing in the lane next to me. They look like the stereotypical college couple everyone wants to be and are simultaneously secretly judging. Seemingly so sickly in love and shit, wrapping around each other as she lets out a laugh and turns into his neck after something he says to her. She's unaware that his gaze is on the outline of an athletic neon green ass as the top half bends to grab a drink out of the short cooler. I roll my eyes. Men are bastards.

"Don't even think about touching it again! Makenzie, why can't you fucking listen?!"

My attention on them is interrupted by the lady standing behind me chastising her daughter. Her voice drips with disdain. It's like nails on a chalkboard to my ears. The vile lady's daughter starts to whimper as my mind drifts while she continues to ridicule her.

Specific memories require a stimulant; they are like the untouchable fine china items reminding me of a dusty, shatter-cracked cream ceramic bowl I remember my mother having as I grew up. It was the focal point quite often as I'd stare and disassociate from what was going on around me or to me. It just sat there looking pretty on the back of the top shelf, only pulled out on less than a handful of occasions. Always, when there was a gathering to exchange fake ass pleasantries or memories about said dead person while floating from small group to group silently gossiping and judging anything from the funeral services to anyone such as the baby who didn't quite look like his supposed daddy. One day, my natural curiosity and defiance had me question the rules. I grabbed the stepladder kept by the side of the refrigerator to climb the shelf and retrieve it…..

The sun shines through the room, glinting off the side, and I am bringing it closer to my face, my fingers placed to start tilting so I can see inside……suddenly I'm being ripped from the top step……

"YOU BETTER NOT DROP IT!!"

"Why can't I hold it? It's so pretty?"

"Rue, give it to me now! I won't ask again!!!"

"But I promise not to drop it."

"If you don't bring your light-bright ass over here right now!"

But I don't move, just stand frozen……I am surprised at the gentleness as she takes it from my hands, almost lovingly, before placing it back in its rightful spot. A look of near stupidity sits on my face as a practically foreign look occupies my mother's. Never have I seen those eyes meet mine with the same warmth, care, or concern.

What doesn't surprise me is the back-handed slap to my face or the fifteen-minute-long, overly exasperated story about it being a precious heirloom from my grandmother. I have always taken the answer as being because the world would go to shit and Cynthia May would roll over in her grave. If I break it, she will break me. Not because it is precious but because it is hers and I am....well, me.

I'm jolted back to reality when the cashier says, "Next." I move forward to pay, inwardly laughing, wondering how many times grandma has been ass up to heaven due to our family as my index finger unconsciously falls from sliding the mosaic-like custom pendant hanging from a delicate white gold chain around my neck. I give the lady behind me a disgusted look, but she doesn't dare say anything. She's embarrassed only about being caught. There would be more tears shed on the way home from the daughter, I'm sure. Usually, I'd be slightly empathetic for the mother because she would probably shed a few of her own as her cries are masked by the running shower. Like I said before, zero fucks to give. The only constant exception, little kids. As fucking annoying as they can be at times, they were innocent.

Handing the young cashier my money, she comments how I must be ready for a makeover or a change from her observation of my items. I respond with an obviously fake smile and tone, "Something like that." It's clear I'm not a customer who will help her pass the time with pleasant chit-chat. With a muttered thanks, I collect my bags and break through the sliding doors. The current thought? *Freedom*.

SEVENTEEN
UNCHAINED PORCELAIN TRINKETS

I hear no breathing,

there will be no more sequels.

Smooth dishes, scattered and spikey,

in front of my feet lies forbidden porcelain.

I'll keep this with me always,

my reminder, a little token.

Mother dearest,
with me forever, you are.

I don't want to be you,
but like you, I am a mar.

EIGHTEEN
BURNT ENDS

"We are all strangers in a strange land, longing for home,
but not quite knowing what or where home is."
-Madeleine L'Engle

LOOKING BACK, LIFE WAS easy when it was void of
color. I have missed the darkness, her welcomed
heaviness, the security blanket my essence longed to be
engulfed in. There is a sense of peace that is inside of
me when I stay on this side. It's my home, my safe
space. I've found that it's only when chasing after the
light that things get complicated. It is not for me. I
thrive in the darkness, relishing in its uncomplicated
yet complete cloaking of perhaps a false world where
you are free to just be. Still, one is at risk of losing all
sight if absent from light for too long. Have I become

blind? The no longer lukewarm but ice-cold water brings me from my internal therapy session as I step from under the water flow and turn the handle. It is no longer flowing. Just dripping remnants of the source remains. Staring down as the last of the water runs down my body, dripping from the peaks and flowing through valleys peppered with fading colors of blues, greens, and yellows, I watch the little black hole swallow it all up. If I stared long enough, would Pennywise come and take me away too? I reach out to the side where I know my towel will hang, sighing slightly when my hand grasps the softness. Wrapping it around my body, it's a stark contrast to the stained, grungy, cheap towels that litter around the floor about my feet.

Out of habit, I reach for a hand towel and fold it into a neat square, lifting it to the mirror and realizing there is no steam on the glass to wipe away. Mother had always insisted on cold showers and baths. Cold showers didn't make me sweat my hair out. Repurposing the little square to rid my exposed skin of the last moisture beads, I then discard the towel down to the cotton graveyard below me. I start unwrapping the waterproof silk bonnet from around my crown, left momentarily stunned as I take my first glance in the mirror. My hair no longer bounces out all over the place, curls landing where they may, stuck in the same shape as they were previously fashioned. It flows straight down, trickling until it stops at the middle of my spine. Watching as I run my hands down the top of my head to the ends, admiring the softness, I focus on my face again and get slightly angry. I'm being tested; I know it. I have failed, but may have just passed the she-devil's finals.

Having been on a natural journey for the last few years, I am pissed to see my hard work down the drain, yet still vain enough to appreciate the softness, sheen, and length I now have. Shrinkage is not an issue anymore as I turn and admire how my hair now falls down the middle of my back. The bright-red color complements my skin tone and causes my eyes to look greener than the standard hazelish color. I hate this color, it reminds me of her, but I love it because it looks better on me. She was too pale. Once I use a specific color or style, I don't return to it a second time. Every transformation is a fresh start. This one is going to be a beautiful disaster.

Walking from the bathroom to cross the room, my breath starts to quicken, but my stride doesn't falter. I refuse to succumb to the dread or remorse I feel, tearing at my defense like a deranged woodpecker, slowly starting to crack through my armor. But with each step closer to the bed, I'm also coming to peace with the fact that my darkness cannot be tamed. That doesn't mean I want to be dancing with the devil just yet.

After all, it wasn't my fault I was invited to the party; I didn't ask to be born into this. I am still determining what comes after or where I shall fall. Making it to the side of the bed, goosebumps start and spread once my thighs connect to the side metal slat of the bed, spreading as my brain starts to process what I'm seeing before me. I gaze at everything but the bed.

"Doooo iiiiiiit nooooooow." I hear the voice echo in my mind. It's like an annoying whisper, but I ignore it while composing myself. Closing my eyes and breathing deeply, I open them to focus their way across the strategically placed items on the reading table to the left of the room as I approach. Feeling a rush of frustration, I push them to the side, sitting down in a huff as I hunch over. One hand resting and draped off my knee, the other hand's index finger tracing the eye-shaped scar inside my right knee. After a few moments of staring down at my big toe while picking at the crack in the wood on the floor, I pause once my eye is drawn to a piece of fabric that is lying by my foot. I halt my picking to run my fingertip along the burnt edges. I fist it and bring it to my nose, holding a false hope that if I breathe in deep enough, I can still smell the faint scent of Sauvage by Christian Dior with forward notes of burnt cotton…..

The devil himself must have entered the room at that moment. I see flashes of colors in my peripheral vision and feel a rising heat prick my skin. I can't bring myself to stop the building of pleasure that is taking over my body, and my eyes close again as it shakes and trembles. I struggle for air when the next sensation I feel is being tossed like a rag doll across the bed onto my stomach. I lie there momentarily, thinking he isn't entirely done with me yet as thoughts of his release never cross my mind; that last ride was all for me.

I hear a commotion followed by, "Oh shit!"

As I turn to look back at him over my shoulder, what catches my eye causes me to stop, wide-eyed. We have knocked his favorite big pillow into the candle next to the bed, which is now on fire. Azrael throws it on the floor and smothers the flames. When he stands, he is panting harder than expected but looks at me with a smirk, laughs a little, and tells me, jokingly, "You owe me a pillow." He heads toward the bathroom. I laugh, but only in the irony.

I hear the water from the sink start to run. There is a part of me that, for a fleeting moment, wishes he was still next to me but our time has come to an end. A few minutes later, there is a thudded silence and a whisper of, "Help," to come and find him. There is no rush on my end; the sound of the water has me in a tranquil state, not quite ready to move on. To start over again. I lie there and shed a tear, instantly mad at myself for believing it could have been any different. At least I got off and had a good laugh. Don't you wish all goodbyes could be this way?

NINETEEN
NIKKI, WHO ARE RUE?

"When I let go of what I am, I become what I might be."
-Laozi

AZRAEL HASN'T CROSSED MY mind in years. Maybe it's a self-preservation thing? It's kept me alive until now. One of my last thoughts of him was after I placed the memento of fabric into the small colorful box. At the time, I could hear the rustle of the items inside as it was placed inside the already labeled, bound for Costa Rica, FcdEx package. As the drop off door shut all those years ago, I wondered if, wherever he headed in his next life, would he end up with the bitch he risked it all for and was going to choose over me? Or, would she be too busy sucking the next dick in line to the gates of Hell to notice him? He hadn't even known my real name, so even if I ran into him in Hell sometime, I'd be as much a stranger sucking his dick, too.

I pulled up IG, double checking I was logged into the correct facade, in an attempt to peg who was meeting Azrael's needs and I didn't have to search long to find the account I was looking for. There she was. Her profile was private, but we were friends. Well, not us, but she and "Nick." There was her fucking face. All beautiful with her perfectly sized broad nose. Big round brown eyes adorned with long thick lashes. A natural body one would use as a reference for plastic surgery. Built by the gods and a face beat to the nines. How did I compare? My hair was straight and stringy, damaged from years of relaxers and bad self-dye jobs. Thinner in the front, probably due to the palm color side of my family. I had dyed it blue-black after Azrael had mentioned my multi-color locs were a distraction from my "pretty face" and he "preferred" straight hair. My compromise was to relax and go dark. In normal lighting, it almost looked like a regular soft black; when my crown hit the sun, the most subtle hint of blue undertones shone through. Blue-black like my battered soul was feeling.

I hadn't seen my natural hair since I was a kid. I changed it periodically through the years. Sometimes years in between, sometimes months, just depended on the occasion. My face was slim and oval, missing the plumpness and fullness I wished for. My nose was small, narrow, and boring. My lips were not paper thin, but nothing to write home about. My smile was decent enough, but my teeth didn't see the light on a regular occasion. My skin was something that I was trying to love but hated. The sun God hadn't blessed me with the most, in my eyes, attractive skin to walk this earth as they did her. I was the shade that was consistently used as a stepping stone for white men who wanted to dip their toes in but still denied the reality of the pool they were dipping into. And by Black men who had fetishized light-skinned women or the occasional decent man who things would seem to be progressing with until it came time to meet the parents. I felt unwanted in both swimming holes. Treatment from women wasn't much better. I tried not to take that so personally, though. We had been hard-wired to hate each other. To be in competition of any and every thing. I just so happened to get hate from both sides. I was privileged yet cursed to walk in my skin. Nothing compared to what my enemy in front of me would endure. But this wasn't about skin. She wanted what was mine and I knew it; an anosmia person could even smell her manipulation and lust for him. I caught myself breathing fast and felt the shaking of my hands. We knew when something was off. I read a quote somewhere by someone who had quickly become one of my favorite people.

I began compiling a list of quotes that seemed to speak to the good inside me. They had become a mantra I would speak daily to ground myself. I tossed the laptop aside and grabbed my phone to pull up my notes. I scrolled and tapped on the words, "Tarryn Fisher Commandments." I needed her words, clutched them like a prized rosary in the hands of sinners during confession, but my brain was having a hell of a tug-o-war match like two of me standing on either side of a brick wall with a hole only big enough for our arms to reach through. They were violently tugging and pulling but making no progress other than bashing each other's faces into a mess. No winners here. I was mentally stuck between heaven and hell, and my demons wouldn't let me go without a fight to the death. Scanning the ever-expanding list, my eyes settled and focused on one; "Live barefoot & fucking fight." I knew the words were not registering in my brain the way she meant, but in that moment, my essence took it literally, and that's just what I would do. Fucking fight.

I picked up the discarded laptop and continued browsing the enemy. She had added a new post earlier that day. A cute picture of her kid, his smiling face beaming at someone out of the frame as he was mid-swing.

-swipe-

A table with too much food for a woman and child.

-swipe-

A close-up selfie with her pristine smile and two outstretched fingers, standing in front of or next to what looked like her TV, based on the dark corner of a square by her chin and the cable that came from her ear.

The caption- "Family is everything. I see good things on the horizon."

What was so fucking good on the horizon? I flipped back and forth through the photos looking for clues until I stopped on one and took a screenshot. I zoomed in on the picture, and I saw it. The table, the food, the fuzzy but recognizable Steelers keychain, and the phone on the counter.

I returned to her page and scrolled to previous posts. Another hiking selfie. Azrael told me she used nature as her therapy. He never went into too much detail with me about her mental health issues, just that she could be unstable. In any other circumstances, I could relate. Hell, we could have even become friends. I'd take your instability and raise you a few pegs off the rocker. Before I even knew what I was doing, I double-clicked the picture and tapped messages. It was time to test how loyal that thought of family was. She clearly wanted to be with him. I hoped, for her sake, she didn't fail because her time with him would decidedly be cut short.

I picked up my phone, going straight for my list. I read each line and repeated them out loud over and over to help drown out the dark inner urges and voices that came from all angles. It was like a dozen Forrest Gump ping-pong champions in my head, all equally good, fighting for the win. What seemed like hours later, the winner was declared.

"Forgive me, Father, for what I'm about to do," I said out loud as a plan developed.

Message - *click*

The rare but normally sweet smile I give feels even more foreign than the Joker expression that followed, imprinting my face as quick but unsteady fingers begin to type….

"Hey Shauna, you are beautiful! I see you like hiking … me too! Have you been to the Rio Valley trails yet? I haven't, but would love to…." My needs would be met by my own design.

Azrael had graduated a few years earlier and was establishing himself in his real-estate career. He was good at it, great with his clients, and always on the go. He never stopped working, even if he was supposed to be off. That never bothered *me, and now it never would. I didn't need to be in a relationship where you were stuck together 24/7. I didn't even need to see your face every day, but I needed communication. I needed reassurance. I needed to feel like I mattered. And he wasn't fulfilling me. I had done my research. I was a student, after all.*

The warm hum of the laptop met my thighs as my eyes hit the open email full of words,

"Nikki,

You've missed your last two sessions. We've talked about this. Please reach-"

I tapped delete before I even finished. I didn't need those appointments. Shit, maybe I did. But I wasn't in the mood to talk about my fucking feelings or be pried into. What had that and countless thousands of dollars gotten me so far?

Index cards laid scattered all around, covering what seems like every inch of the bed, desk, and floor. Poster boards and graphs, push pinned, perfectly aligned, and spaced equally, covered the chipped beige walls. Open binders and overly highlighted notebooks were propped up on the floor against the bed. It all added color to the otherwise bland room. I threw them in a fit of rage when I couldn't remember the simple answer to who the Father of Ecology was after the third round of self-quizzing. Alexander von Humbolt, how fucking hard was that? Finals were around the corner and my perfectionist brain was determined to get an "A." I was only a semester away from finishing my Bachelor of Biology degree at the University of Texas Rio Grande Valley, and an A on my finals in this Ecology course would secure my spot in a six week, student-led ecological-based tour in Costa Rica during summer break. I'd get to combine my love of nature, gardening, and science all in one. If I was being honest, the only problem with this plan was that I could grow increasingly frazzled and would begin to self-sabotage with this much pressure. My deep anxiety had been creeping in ever since I realized I would have to dispose of my boyfriend and that I would have three upcoming finals all in the same day. The best way for me to study was by playing teacher; he was usually my student. It gave me a sense of control of the situation and allowed me to clearly see where I lacked in retaining information. But, my student has to be eliminated.

HONK! HONK!

A traffic pissing contest brings me out of my trance of the recent past. Blinking hard, I glance around the open-air ice cream shop tucked right on the ocean. My research team is stopped in the city for the day before we head out to the last of our adventure in Costa Rica. Nobody got me this opportunity, I earned this shit. The bit of consolation cash from Azrael was earned, too. Once I shed myself of his and Shauna's dead weight, my professors allowed me to retake my exams. They understood I was going through a difficult time and just panicked. My genuine tears for fear of failure convinced them I was the model student who earned her second chance. It wasn't my fault my boyfriend had died, I was simply a sad girlfriend. Now, I'm finishing up my six week, turned twelve week, ecological research expedition, hence, extending my plans. I tell them I'll meet them back at the hostel; I want to use the faster internet and check some emails. That is only a partial lie. Most everyone in our small group of ten are vegan, vegetarian, or anti-sugar. I am stuck with health nuts and I want to be gluttonous and confess my sins in peace. My ice cream has become soup. Well, shit.

Powering up my phone, I log into IG first, clicking over to my personal profile to check Father's page and download all the #TWT screenshots that a few of my fellow PLNs kept me updated on while I've been busy with the research trip. I attempt to somewhat branch out, just not of my own accord. The PLNs are pesky, determined bitches who never stop checking in, no matter how long they are ignored. I pop in and out of my account at will, and no one bats an eye, no need for an explanation. They would never know who I was during other random interactions. To all of them, I am always Rue. Other versions of myself, such as Nikki Melton, came and went as momentary fans who lurked the page so other eyes could never see through the lies. Having two profiles made it easier to keep things separate, but Nikki won't exist once I am done here. Maybe my time as Nikki coming to a close will help me be better, maybe it won't, but I am ready to go with the flow. "Be like water," the tide comes in and out consistently. One of the newest lessons learned from my #TWT catch-up session.

Taking a smiling selfie where I sit, I turn to catch the water behind me. My head is void of lengthy hair, short dark brown corkscrew curls replace the long straight phase. Halle Berry, back in the day, length. I am embracing who I am—trying to anyway.

Leaning into the good and healing some wounds. I have a new therapist lined up, too. After Azrael passed from an "unexpected" heart attack months ago, I decided I needed to shit or get off the pot. Going all in on trying to be the best version of Rue since I am approved for transfer from UTRGV to Virginia Commonwealth University and set to start in three weeks.

I walk back to the hostel and see some street dogs mulling around in the sand. One looks to have an animal bone of some sort in a tug-of-war match with its companion. The scenic portrait behind them has my mind once more wandering to water....and wondering if bones float.

Sitting back in my solo occupant room, the colorful little box by the keyboard catches my eye just as someone's cigar smoke wafts in through the open window. The blowing cream curtains do nothing to stop the smell. It is distinct and earthy, with a hint of sweetness and spice; not enjoyable and my nostrils flare at the stink. The little trinkets in my box jar around as I unlock and push back the lid. The little piece of fabric is in my fingers as I bring it to my nose and inhale deeply. I can still smell the char. My other hand lifts my phone, still open on my IG page. I move the little notification, "Post Uploaded," still at the bottom of the screen out of the way so I can see the caption.

#RVA #VCU #Newbeginnings

TWENTY
SEEK AND YOU SHALL FIND

"The color of truth is gray."
-Andre Gide

NO HAPPINESS.

No sadness.

No rage.

Blank.

Darkness.

And yet, even in this space, I see clearly for the first time. Night vision.

I have lost it, but I am found.

I try not to look up as I walk down the crowded sidewalk, heading home from my quick trip to the corner store that's less than a block away. I fucking forgot to get my Backwoods cigars to roll with tonight while I was out earlier. Walking through the crowd of people, I see her face everywhere. Every fair-skinned woman is her, and she wants me. She is partially the reason I even exist, and she is still the bane of my existence.

Even void of oxygen in her lungs, she keeps taunting me, torturing me, tipping the scale in her favor. She makes sure I believe I am nothing, but her misfortune was when I began to believe I can be something. That is even worse. Believing you are something, but still end up like nothing. The damn rug being pulled from under your feet time and time again. My bones ache from having to pick myself up so many times. My soul is angry. She is tired.

TWENTY-ONE
MY OWN WORST ENEMY

"Life is that perfect fine line between ironies."
-Serj Tankian

I TAKE A LONG hit of the ever-shrinking blunt. The rolled leaf in hand is moving, but there is no wind. I watch the ash fall from the tip, hit the table, and disintegrate into a pile. The pieces slowly blow away as the oscillating fan turns in my direction, swirling up and mixing with the dust particles floating in the air. Ashes to ashes, dust to dust…..

My mood is excited and fearful, but not enough to be deterred. There is a sense of peace in the presence of death. Fingers trembling, and with slight hesitation, the pill is lifted to my lips. Exhaling deeply, allowing all the smoke to escape before I place it in between my left cheek and bottom row of teeth. Turning to walk to Wyant's bedside, the capsule feels tacky and sticks to my cheek tissue as I push it down farther and back with my tongue.

In the last few minutes, Wyant's body has gone from breathing hard and fast to struggling for each breath. Before me, every breath's entire cycle is like watching a thunderstorm. Each wheezing inhale, the lightning of life, 1…2…3…4. The thunder is moving farther away with every rattled exhale. I lift the cup and take in the mouthful of liquid, swallowing hard; the "gluck" sound bounces off the walls like an echo. Placing the glass on the nightstand, I face the bed; eyes scan up and down his body, zoning in on how his abdomen contorts with each desperate inhale and exhale. His chest looks sunken. Every deep-gasping wheeze now becomes more desolate. His futile attempts to lift his head cause it to sink like dead weight further into the pillow like a Venus flytrap, ever so slowly closing in and around its prey... It's almost time.

I crawl onto the bed, laying on my side and enveloping myself partially across his still naked body. My leg slides across his thigh, bent snuggly into the empty space between his own. My face on the pillow next to his, I turn my Wyant's head to face mine, meeting his now almost black, sunken, dull eyes. They stare back at me, filled with what seems like regret, confusion, and fear. A soft sound leaves his lips, causing my eyes to look down. They are dry and peeling like a drought-stricken mud crack begging Mother Nature to cry upon its surface. I cradle his face, the damp skin rippling under my thumb as I caress his cheek. "I'll love you always, even in death," the words sound choked as I gently place my lips against his. He never inhales again, as if I were also cursed as the angel of death in the flesh.

I start to feel funny. I need to get moving, return to the table. I am moving slower, taking what feels like an eternity to collect and organize all the tossed-aside items and my colorful box. I open the lid, remove the final contents, and carefully lay each item in the shape of a cross on the center of the table, wanting all the people I ever loved in my presence; I don't need to speak words. I can feel them all around me; mixed thoughts of both being embraced or enslaved into their existence send my mind racing. They may not love me anymore, but I will no longer be walking through the fire alone. We'll be one big family of fucked-upness together.

I sit drinking the cheap ass whiskey straight from the bottle until I can feel the warmth taking over my body while staring quietly back and forth between the bed and the table in front of me. Breaking the seal of the small airtight bag, I pour the contents onto the table, breaking up what's there and filling the last little brown leaf. Going extra slow since my vision is starting to blur, my twitchy hands making the usually routine task feel like even my own body is fucking sick of me.

A short, despondent chuckle comes out as I bring my hand up to my mouth, the other lighting the flame. This blunt and I are one and the same. Each person had taken their consumption until there was nothing left but the glowing roach carelessly discarded, desperately sucking at the oxygen to keep itself lit.

Puff Puff - Pass… Puff Puff - Pass… Only this time, I got the last hit.

PINGGGG.

Wyant's phone on the table lets off an email alert sounding like bombs going off in the quiet room. My hands are reaching before I even realize it. Clumsily, I enter his password. My finger taps the two twin melting seas of blue and white. I open the newest email, pulling the phone away from my eyes to be able to make out words.

To: Wyant Minnick

From: Karen Cracky

Subject: YOU'RE GOING TO LOVE IT, COME AND GET IT!!!

My head throws back, and I swear my mother's laugh echoes from my lips. I fucking knew I was right! And a fucking Karen at that…. Ironic how the universe had to fuck me one last solid time. I should have gone after her first. Hadn't planned it this way; I regret the order of my impulses and lack of thorough planning. She should have gotten hers, too. She belongs with us. I bring the screen back into view, and my eyes have to re-read what it says several times before my increasingly useless pink organ catches up.

Wyant-

It's ready!!! It's beautiful and I think Rue is going to love it! I attached pictures below. Let me know what you think! We have a small window for any changes before you leave, but it's absolutely perfect if you ask me. Let me know when you want to come in! I'll be out of town next week, but Mike will be here to assist.

Have a great time on your trip if I don't see you before and preemptive congrats! Thank you again for entrusting us with creating this unique piece.

-K

Attached are two pictures. My heart squeezes as I'm zooming in on the small pictures. Once it clicks, placing all the puzzle pieces, my breath catches and a choked gasp escapes me. Wyant was paying attention to my endless ramblings of Father and my, at her fault, obsession with blue lights. "Airport Fucking Blue" is the official name. A medium-sized flawless blue stone of the perfect shade sits encased in a thin band of what looks like broken chains.

The second photo is a 4x4 square montage of the inscription around the inside of the band.

A blue light wrapped in chains no more, my Duckie forever, you are.

My heart is beating faster than I have ever experienced before. Like I have taken every upper known to man and was coming down fast, ready to crash and fade.

WHAT THE FUCK DID I DO!?!?

Visions of exploding blue lights come crashing in waves. Nothing makes sense anymore. The phone wants to make out with the table, so I tighten my grip. My finger presses four times on what I hope are the right buttons, then place the phone back on the table.

HE WANTS TO MARRY ME!

HE LOVES ME!!! Wants to marry me! He loves me! WYANT!!

My caged internal music box provides the only acoustics I can hear as I lay like a doll in the chair, head to the side. I'm not even vaguely aware of the pool of liquid and bottle that lie at my feet until it's too late. *Lay down......Go to him.*

The room is spinning as I attempt to stand, losing my balance as I step. All I see is the floor rapidly approaching. My arms don't even attempt to break my fall, landing with a thud, but I don't feel a thing. I must have yanked my chain in the process because I can see it has flown across the floor near the nightstand by Wyant's bedside. I internally laugh, if only Mother were in front of me now. I roll onto my back, legs sprawled out, staring at the ceiling, the cool floor calling to me. I'm just what she said I'd be; good for nothing but on my back, legs open. Only, I couldn't get my knees to my head if I tried.

Wet warmness starts at my waist, slowly spreading once the blue cotton fabric has had its fill. My sight is beginning to fade.....*WAKE UP!!!!* Whaling and waning sounds disturb the slumber my whole being is craving. Slowly rolling to my side, I can see the bed, but it feels a mile away. I need to get to Wyant. I want to lay in his arms one more time. I need to tell him I am sorry!! As I try to roll, my necklace appears, summoning me. I can't do this without it. I slowly make my way across the floor. Crawling, each movement feels as though the distance is still multiplying. I gather I have made it to my destination when the only thing keeping me from falling forward is my face against a hard object, the small brass handle feeling cool on my forehead. My body gives in and I, again, find myself sprawled on the floor, stomach down and face to the side. Using what little strength I have left, screaming in agony as the fire is taking over the inside of my being, I keep trying to pull myself up on the bed. It's not a mission my body can complete. I can feel my body shutting down….

"WYYYYYYAAAAANNNNTTTTT!!!"

I panic, but everything is in slow motion. I catch sight of his lifeless outstretched hand hanging from the side like he himself was here to help as he always was. As I try to maneuver myself closer to him, I can't make it the final few feet. This final collapse has me on my side. My fist relinquishes the necklace once again. I watch helplessly as it slides under the bed. I can't reach it, but I use the last energy I have left holding me to the world to reach my hand out toward him as everything starts to fade. He won't be waiting for me after all. Will any of them??

As my eyes close, my mother's laughing face flashes before me. It's okay, though. She thinks she's won. I have nothing left to lose. Can't wait to meet this bitch at the gates of Hell. She created this monster, but I have learned to outplay the master. I lost the repeated game of chess but gained knowledge of all her moves and strategies. I will make her life in Hell feel like she'd been in heaven before my arrival. She may have

"Rued" the day I was born, but she is going to deplore the day I die.

The excruciating pain exploding through my chest causes my body to contort and writhe. My body spasms and locks, bent backwards like an exorcism is being performed but there is no evil spirit left to banish from my body; we are now one. My eyes fly open as the life starts to leave my body, as the rightside-up canvas painting of the Queen peers down at her Judas, bathed in rapidly changing hues of red and blue. I betrayed her, I betrayed them. I betrayed him. But, I too am deceived, this isn't all on me.

My final thoughts come as ragged whispers and colors seem to be melting into a liquid mass of darkness....

"Forgive...1...2... me Father ..1...2...3...4 for all 1...2..our...1 si———-.

EPILOGUE
BROKEN COMMANDMENTS

TWO YEARS LATER ...

IT IS HOTTER THAN hell out here. Miss Ruby got me running around, getting the last of the scoops out for the day. That's right, I cleaned up. I cleaned up and Ruby offered me work helping out anywhere I'm needed at Ruby Scoops. Up front scooping, in the back keeping the kitchen clean, you name it and I'll be glad to do it.

Man, Rue is something else. That woman up and moved on with her man I suppose. No call, no visit, nothing. But one thing she did do, well, I suppose she left what she couldn't take with her and what she thought I could use. All packed into a few big ol' boxes with an envelope labeled "Ronnie" sitting in the backseat of her beat up 1997 two door Honda Accord that she parked across the street from the overpass that I called home back then. That girl is a ninja or sumthin' though, I swear. I was confused as hell wakin' up trapped under a thickass blanket that wasn't there the night before. I didn't even wake up when she tucked the key into the bended edge of my beanie. She knew it's where I kept my chapstick for easy access.

The box had a lot of her favorite clothing items covered in that damn cult she rambled on about sometimes. Now why she go and leave all that? I just hope she's not in some kinda trouble. Her favorite glass smoking pipes and bongs were the next to come out and left sitting on its side was a scrapbook; filled with notes, doodles, and poetry. The cover only said,

"Poetry is nothing but the insight into our sins and souls."

Flipping through briefly, there were items heavily secured with clear tape on each page. One had a background of a picture collage of what looked like some trail in the woods, then what looked like a piece of rock with dark paint splattered or somethin' and had been secured with tape on the edge of the page. There was a poem in the middle that made no sense to me, somethin' about how much she liked hiking, I guess. It felt like I was invading, so I closed it and put it aside in the closet. Haven't touched it since. Her thoughts are safe with me.

Boy, she left me a pretty penny, too. Inside that envelope was twelve thousand dollars in cash. Now I know Rue would never bring trouble to my door. I know that money's clean. Crisp hundred dollar bills. I don't know what game she's playing at but I sure do appreciate a part in it. I took that cash and set myself straight with a trip to The Trio's barber shop and to Walmart for some fresh work clothes to present myself in. Stepped foot into my first "Tar-jay," as the youngins call it. Those damn coffees are too expensive, but I sure got myself two of 'em and cake on a stick before I left.

Ruby sends me off with a fresh scoop of Rue's favorite, my paycheck, and I head to *my* car. Yeah, she left me her ride, too. Can you believe that shit? Not much to look at, but gets me where I need to go. I can deliver groceries to anyone who needs - keep the tradition going, paying it forward or whatever. When I get home, I reach into the glove compartment for my check. It sticks to something that pulled out with it when I tugged.

"Rio Valley Trails Weekly Pass. Please display in vehicle. Paid : CASH. Valid from 6/11/15-6/18/15,"

I read aloud before crumbling into my fist, tossing it into the trash, and walking into my house.

THE END

FATHER FISHER'S
TEN COMMANDMENTS

1. "Love is religion"
2. "What you wrap around your soul determines your outcome"
3. "Mute & Live"
4. "Live barefoot & fucking fight"
5. "You'll feel me in the fall backwards."
6. "Women hold all the power. They should use it as a whip, not offer it up like a sacrifice."
7. "You don't forgive because they deserve it. You forgive to keep your heart soft."
8. "Fortune favors the brave"
9. "Fuck fear"
10. "You are a blue light wrapped in chains. Break them."

ALL THE "COMMANDMENTS" HAVE been said by the real life "Father," Tarryn Fisher, throughout her amazing books (seriously, go read them after this!) or communications with readers/followers, and they really can help you during challenging times. I know they have, for not only myself, but countless others including her devout following of readers. We call ourselves a girl gang/cult - *Passionate Little Nutcases*. Some have been affirmations said on a daily basis for weeks/months until I could believe them. Others, I am still on my journey with and that's okay!

Yes, I'm obsessed, but not like "Fig" level obsessed. If my daughter's name, the majority of the physical books on my shelves, and the *PLN/TF* gear I'm usually sporting along with the tattoos on my arm don't show my level of ride-or-die for this woman and crew, I think this story gave it away, lol. In the end, I hope her words help lift you and serve as a beacon of light and my words you see as a warning; staying in the darkness can rob you of all the light you deserve. Follow the North Star!

#WWTFD

Playlist for "Rotten Fruit"

https://tinyurl.com/373y59y8

Darkness by Eminem
Family Portrait by Pink
Wake Me Up Inside by Evanescence
Janie's Got a Gun by Aerosmith
Jolene cover by Pentatonix X Dolly Parton
Thinking Out Loud by Ed Sheeran
Just Give Me A Reason by Pink
Man In The Mirror by Michael Jackson
Oh My God by Adele
Maneater cover by Hall & Oates
Read Between The Lines by Aaliyah
Stranger In My House by Deborah Cox
Don't Hurt Yourself by Beyonce
Mr. Brightside by The Killers
Numb by Linkin Park
Mad Woman by Taylor Swift
Runnin' (Lose it All) by Beyonce
I Told You I Was Mean by Elle King
People by Libianca
(One of Those) Crazy Girls by Paramore
Self Sabotage by Rebbeca Black
Haunted by Beyonce
Broken Glass by Rachel Platten
Disturbia by Rhianna
Heartbreak Hotel by Whitney Houston
I get so lonely by Janet Jackson
Cage Fighter (remaster) by TWWO
Cinderella's Dead by Emeline

ROTTEN FRUIT

Ultralight Beam by Stan Walker
Me, Myself and I by Beyonce

ACKNOWLEDGEMENTS

FIRST AND FOREMOST, TO my Panda. I love you for the next 27 years *wink*. Thank you for helping to rebuild my heart and soul piece by piece, even when it has meant giving a piece of yours. Thank you for loving me when I can't love myself. For loving our boys the way you do and giving me our Tarryn Olivia.

My minis, my babies- Sebastian, Silas, and Tarryn Olivia. Mommy loves you more than you know. I am always proud of you. This was for you as much as it was for me. A part of healing needed in steps to become a better mother that I know I can be and that you deserve. May you know I have always tried and always will. If you ever read this in the future, please don't think I murdered anyone, lol. I vow to always protect, uplift, and enrich your lives with love and joy to the best of my ability.

To Cat and Leeah, my heartbeats, my sisters from other misters. Part of my A1s. Y'all pushed me every step of the way. My life hasn't been the same since you two came in. You brought life back into me. Enough said. I'll hold in my "extraness" here to spare Cat's eyes. Lol. I tell you both daily. You know. #Trio4Life and to our Lee Anne. You are ours and we love you.

Everyone needs a Windy. I will wander with you forever, as long as it ain't back to that hotel from hell.

To Tarryn Fisher and the Passionate Little Nutcases. Y'all saved me. Literally. I love you bitches. My forever tribe and Queen. May we frolic in shadows and dance in the sun together forever. #PLN4Life

My Terry Rock, the most kick ass, phenomenal librarian, a scrawny, troubled soul with a love of reading and the best a school could have. I hid many days in your office. You were (and still are) a refuge for quite a few of us through those years. We misfits trying to find our way but hiding from life and the world. You supplied me with endless books, words of encouragement and still, 'til this day, love and friendship. I love you forever. You truly have been my rock.

To my editors who I'm proud to call friends, Ash and Al, you took a chance on me and made every step of this process a joy. Your enthusiasm and dedication to your authors shows in every interaction and detail from day one and beyond the end. Forever my book "aunties," I love you. Grateful for you both.

Traci MF'n Finlay and THE Renita Lofton McKinney, my loves, my mentors from afar. It was a dream to have your eyes read this story. Thank you for your invaluable feedback, but mostly, thank you for loving, supporting, and believing in me. I couldn't have gotten this far, or had the courage to publish, without you both.

My Rotten Alphas- Abigail R., Amanda B., Bobbi H., Jenny B., Tasara V.,Vicky S., and Ziah K. You ladies are amazing and I couldn't have asked for a better alpha crew! The amount of support, love, and honesty you poured into me during this process will not be forgotten.

Virginia, Jovana, and Murphy; thank you for putting up with my chaos and helping to proofread, format, and dress my first "book baby."

Last, my ARC readers and team members. For every message, text, call, review, video, kind word you have sent me, I will never forget. I am so grateful you took the chance on a newbie and her words. I love you.

Mic Drop

www.ingramcontent.com/pod-product-compliance
Lightning Source LLC
Chambersburg PA
CBHW051952170626
46808CB00007B/2580